GARY SOTO

OFF AND RUNNING

Illustrated by Eric Velasquez

SCHOLASTIC INC.
New York   Toronto   London   Auckland   Sydney
Mexico City   New Delhi   Hong Kong   Buenos Aires

Text copyright © 1996 by Gary Soto.
Illustrations copyright © 1996 by Eric Velasquez.
All rights reserved.
Published by Scholastic Inc., 557 Broadway, New York, NY 10012,
by arrangement with Delacorte Press, an imprint of Random House
Children's Books, a division of Random House, Inc.
Printed in the U.S.A.

ISBN 0-439-58047-1

1 2 3 4 5 6 7 8 9 10   40   12 11 10 09 08 07 06 05 04 03

OFF AND
RUNNING

CHAPTER 1

Miata Ramirez stopped working on her fifth-grade math when the speaker on the wall crackled and hissed. She put down her pencil and blew the eraser rubbings from her paper. She sucked in a lot of air and blew again, sending the rubbings off the top of her desk. They fell to the floor like black snow.

The speaker crackled, hissed, and finally popped. The school principal, Mr. Rios, was ready to make his daily announcements. His voice was as thick as a frog's.

"Good morning, students," he greeted them.

Miata looked up at the speaker and mouthed, "*Buenos días.*"

The principal cleared his throat. He announced the canned-food drive, the *folklórico* sign-ups, the baseball card swap meet, and the soccer practice after school. He mentioned the special visitor on Thursday, Señor Gomez the Magnificent, and the fifth-grade field trip to the zoo. He informed the students that two jackets had been found on the playground. "One of them has three dollars in change," he added.

Everybody's hands shot up. "Oh, it's my jacket. It's mine!"

Mrs. Diaz, the teacher, told them to settle down, which they did.

Mr. Rios announced the spelling bee and the PTA meeting. Then he sneezed loudly.

"*Salud*," Miata mouthed. She couldn't help noticing that the flag of the United States near the speaker moved. Strong sneeze, she thought.

"And congratulations to Rudy Herrera for collecting the most aluminum cans," Mr. Rios continued after a moment. He announced that Rudy had won the baseball autographed by Barry Bonds, slugger for the San Francisco Giants.

Miata winced. She had wanted the baseball

badly. She had never gotten an autograph from anyone famous. Her one autograph was from Ronald McDonald, who she knew was really her cousin Manuel in costume.

"He's lucky," Miata said to herself. She imagined Rudy on the school grounds, tossing the ball up and down, up and down, almost showing off. He would probably add his name to the baseball— Barry Bonds and Rudy Herrera.

The principal sneezed a second time and then announced the fall elections for school officers. He explained the school tradition allowing only fifth-graders to run for president and vice president. And only this grade was allowed to vote, since they were the oldest students in their school. He mentioned that Miata Ramirez and Ana Avila from room 6 had decided to run for the top offices.

"From room eight," Mr. Rios continued, "we have two more candidates . . . Rudy Herrera for prez and Alex Garcia for vice prez."

Miata lifted her eyebrows as she turned to Ana, sitting two seats to her left.

"Rudy and Alex?" Miata mouthed.

"Yes, Rudy and Alex," Mr. Rios replied, anticipating the school's disbelief. The boys were known as goofy kids on and off the playground. Only last week they had come to school wearing mismatched shoes—a red tennis shoe on one foot and a black tennis shoe on the other.

The speaker crackled, hissed, and popped and then went silent.

Miata shook her head and continued with her math problems. A new herd of eraser rubbings quickly gathered on her desk. But her mind began to wander. It kept returning to the school elections. She recalled that three of her cousins in Los Angeles—Veronica, Lalo, and Rosie—had won their school elections. It's in my blood, she figured. I'm meant for politics. This might be the beginning of something big.

When the recess bell rang, Miata and Ana, the best of friends and now running mates in the school elections, hurried out of their classroom.

"Can you believe it?" Miata asked as she led Ana toward the slides. "We have to run against Rudy and Alex."

Ana was smaller than Miata. She was small

4

enough to pass for a third-grader. But she was quick, and as bright as a flashlight beaming three inches from your face. She was loyal, too. When Miata had asked Ana if she wanted to be her running mate, Ana had shouted, *"Claro que sí."* She thought that Miata meant going out for the track team. But Miata gave her the lowdown about the school elections. Ana froze with worry, a finger in her mouth like a carrot.

"Why do you want to run?" Ana asked.

Ana's question had given Miata momentary pause. She knew that she wanted to do something big, a selfish reason by itself. She turned this question over and over like a coin. Did she have something to give to the school, or was she clamoring for popularity? As if it were homework, she decided to save the hard question until later.

"Just because it would be neat to try to win," Miata finally answered Ana.

It was recess. Ana and Miata stood alone on the school grounds.

"I know. Everybody likes them, but I think we can beat them," Ana said. She bit into her apple and chewed it like a rabbit.

"We have to think about a plan, Ana," Miata said.

Miata explained that they should make posters and buttons. She said they should try to get the votes of the girls and some of the more intelligent boys. She was explaining her strategy when a knot of kids approached them. Rudy was among them, along with Alex, whose shoelaces were flopping about his feet.

"Miata!" Rudy called. He was tossing his Barry Bonds baseball into the air and whistling "Take Me Out to the Ball Game."

"What?" Miata asked as she sized up Rudy and Alex. They were wearing jeans with streaks of green on the knees. The collars of their T-shirts were stretched from being yanked when the boys wrestled on the grass.

"I want to wish you luck on your campaign," Rudy said, licking his lips. He spit out a mouthful of shelled sunflower seeds. When he extended his hand, Miata gave it a shake.

"You're gonna need luck, too," Ana said. "You and Alex."

"That's cool," Alex said, butting in. His face was fat with a sugar doughnut. He swallowed, smacked his lips, and cleared his throat. "After all, we don't got nothing against you."

"Yeah, we like you. Huh, Alex?" Rudy agreed brightly. He snapped his fingers and said, "In fact, we like you so much that I'll let you hit my baseball."

"I don't want to hit your baseball." Miata turned away. A dark cloud of anger crossed her face. She wished the boys would leave.

"Come on, Miata." Rudy stuffed his face with a handful of sunflower seeds. "I bet you can hit it . . . if I pitch underhand."

"Miata's a good hitter, Rudy. You know she is," Ana said.

Miata turned and faced Rudy. She heard the challenge in Rudy's voice. She glanced down at the baseball. Hitting a baseball with Barry Bonds's signature would be a good way to start off her campaign. Students might hear about it or, better yet, see that ball sail over the fence. Everyone would be awed by her strength.

"Let's try it, dude," she said simply.

"Smack it one," Ana whispered. She punched her tiny fist into her tiny palm.

The knot of kids hurried to the scraggly field, which was wet from the sprinklers.

Miata took a bat that was as tall as Ana and almost as heavy. With a grunt, she swung it to her shoulder and gave it a swing. The weight of the bat nearly pulled her off balance.

"The bat's too heavy," Miata complained as she looked around. "Don't we have another bat?"

"A heavy bat is better," Rudy argued as he rubbed the ball in his hands. "You can hit really hard with it."

Miata turned the bat over and examined it closely. She gripped it tightly, then loosely. She spit in her palms and rubbed them together. She placed the bat on her shoulder, thinking that perhaps the weight would help her hit the ball far. She was ready.

The kids stood back and gave Miata room. Rudy took the mound. He breathed in, then wound up and tossed the baseball underhand.

Miata swung wildly and missed, nearly falling

over from the weight of the bat. Alex called, "Strike one," as he retrieved the baseball. He threw it back to Rudy and cheered, "Nice pitch, homes."

Miata stepped back into the batter's box. She inhaled and set the bat back on her shoulder. She swung and missed again.

"Good try," Rudy said with a smirk.

"Keep your compliments to yourself," Miata hollered.

Miata winked at Ana as if to say, "Watch this."

Rudy went through a series of ridiculous windup motions, his pitching arm whirling like an airplane propeller. Finally he stopped and grinned. He pitched the ball, which left his fingers as slowly as a cloud.

The baseball shot like a rocket off Miata's bat. It sailed over a tall shrub, two trees, three telephone wires, and six sparrows perched on the wires. It landed on the roof of the main school building.

"How was that, Rudy?" Miata teased. She threw down the bat, spanking her palms free of dust and sweat. She looked around at the spectators and yelled, "Don't forget to vote for me!"

"You can hit pretty far," Rudy mumbled, his face fat with another handful of sunflower seeds. "What about my ball?"

"Don't worry, Rudy," Miata said. "I'll get the ball for you."

With Ana in the lead, Miata ran to the building. She grabbed on to a drainpipe and boosted herself onto the roof. She stood on the roof, excited. She could see Mrs. Diaz in the distance and the principal, Mr. Rios. He was shooting baskets with third-graders.

"Great view," she said to herself.

Just then, as she swatted her palms, which were embedded with bits of grainy asphalt, the bell rang. Recess was over. The kids scattered toward their classes, leaving only Rudy, Alex, and Ana yelling, "Hurry up! Get the ball! We gotta go!"

Miata hurried as she searched the roof. She found a Frisbee, which she tossed down, and a deflated air mattress, which she turned over like a blanket. What's this doing here? she wondered. With her hand shading her eyes, she scanned the roof. A mustache of sweat slowly grew on her upper lip.

11

By the time she found the ball, close to the air-conditioning unit, everyone had hurried off, even Ana. Miata was alone. Her legs shook like a wobbly table.

"I'm in trouble," she whispered. She looked at the edge of the roof. Sitting down, she scooted toward the edge until her legs dangled. It was easier climbing up than getting down. Her heart was racing. The mustache of sweat was now a full-grown beard.

Minutes passed. Miata knew that everyone in class was working on social studies. Ana was probably cowering while Mrs. Diaz looked around the room, asking about Miata.

"Stupid ball," Miata said to the baseball in her hands. She studied the autograph of Barry Bonds but looked up when she heard her name. It was Mr. Rios's voice, but now it wasn't coming over the loudspeaker. He was standing below, hands on hips and shaking his head. "What are you doing up there!"

Dime-sized tears filled her eyes. She didn't know how to explain it to him. Through a glaze of tears, she saw the janitor approach with an aluminum ladder. She turned and looked over her shoulder when she heard a sparrow chirp. The bird was sitting on the deflated air mattress, apparently resting. Then it beat its wings and flew away. Miata wished she could do the same.

"I'm disappointed in you!" Mr. Rios scolded.

"Me too," Miata said.

Now she would have to climb down that ladder and into the angry heat of the principal's office—not a great way to start a campaign for student body president.

Miata and Ana kicked through the fall leaves, which were the color of copper pennies. The afternoon sun was dipping over the rooftops of houses as a gentle wind stirred the trees. At almost every house they passed, a cat slept in the last remnants of sunlight. October was upon them, but Miata could think about only one thing—the embarrassment of getting caught on the roof of the school. She had had to do some quick talking before Mr. Rios cooled down. He had gripped the seams of the baseball so hard that he smudged the signature. Now it said " arry Bonds."

Miata stepped over the cracks in the sidewalk and said, "I should have known better."

"I'm sorry for leaving you up there," Ana said. She was upset with herself—a true best friend would have stayed with Miata when the recess bell rang. "Did Mr. Rios yell at you?"

"Nah, he just said over and over how disappointed he was with me." Miata looked down at the sidewalk and then over at downcast Ana. "Don't look so sad, Ana. There was nothing you could do."

Miata left Ana at the corner. She turned and, walking backward, yelled, "We'll beat those boys." Ana waved and yelled back, "See you tomorrow."

Miata hurried home, her ponytail whipping about and her backpack slapping the wings of her shoulders with the weight of her books. She was breathless, not from running but from the thought of running for office. She was determined to win. Unlike the previous president of the school, Marcos Mendoza, a handsome boy with green eyes but lazier than a sleepy cat, Miata wanted to accomplish things.

As she leaped up the steps of her porch, her younger brother called, "Miata! Look what I found."

She turned to Joey, who was smiling. His front baby teeth were gone and in their place his tongue, as pink as bubble gum, wiggled. He held up a small white box.

"It's pretty scary," Joey said.

"What is it?"

Miata shrugged off her backpack and approached her brother.

"It might give you lots of ugly nightmares."

"Let me see." Miata was now curious.

"You might throw up," Joey warned, his tongue wiggling as wildly as a worm.

"Yeah, sure," Miata said. She made a face at her brother. "Joey, stop doing that with your tongue! *¡Es feo!*" She looked closely at the box. "All right. Let me see."

Joey's tongue slipped back into his mouth. He raised the box and slowly pulled off the lid. Sitting in the box on white gauze was a child's index finger with what looked like dried blood.

"I found it in the alley," Joey said, a smile at the corner of his mouth. "I think it's still alive."

The finger wiggled like Joey's tongue. It wiggled again and raised itself up like a snake.

"It's alive," Joey said in a hushed voice. His eyes were big, and his mouth hung open like a sack. "I think it's centuries old but alive!"

The finger began to curl and then moved from side to side. It began to tap against the gauze.

"It's trying to tell us something!" Joey said. "It's an ancient message."

"Sorry, Joey, but I learned that trick when I was five years old."

The finger quivered and went dead as Joey looked up at his sister.

Miata knew that the finger in the box was Joey's finger. He had cut out a hole in the bottom of the box and stuck in his finger. Then he had smeared ketchup around the fingernail and the knuckle.

Miata smiled at Joey. She asked, "Is Mom home?"

"She's in the backyard," Joey said, pointing with the finger that was still in the box. He took it out and licked off the ketchup.

Miata jumped off the porch and went around to the backyard, where her mother was pulling up the dead tomato plants.

"Mom!" Miata greeted her.

17

"How was school, *mi'ja*?" her mother asked. She slapped the dirt off her palms and gave her daughter a hug.

"Fine," Miata said. She helped her mother tug loose two more scraggly tomato plants and stuff them into a plastic garbage bag. Brushing the dirt from her hands, Miata announced, "Mom, I'm running for office."

"*¿Qué?*" her mother said, confused. She was lifting a garbage bag to carry to the alley. "What's that?"

Miata explained as she followed her mother to the alley. She told Mrs. Ramirez that she and Ana were going to run for school office. Miata said that if you were elected, you could make changes at school.

"Sounds important," Miata's mother said. "But first I think you better change into your play clothes."

"Mom, this is serious!"

"I'm serious, too." With a grunt, her mother heaved the garbage bag into the gray, elephant-sized Dumpster. "You keep ripping up your knees."

Miata looked down at her knees, which were grass stained from playing soccer with the boys at school. She had to admit that her mother was right.

Miata hurried inside the house, sniffing the delicious smell of *chile verde* on a back burner. Using a towel, she lifted the lid and looked in at the meat and green peppers piping like lava. Hunger filled her mouth.

"Mom's the best cook," she concluded as she lowered the lid back onto the pan. She hurried off to her bedroom.

Evening slowly descended as Miata made posters that said VOTE FOR MIATA AND ANA. Using construction paper, she cut out heart-shaped badges that said MIATA AND ANA. She pinned one to her blouse, admired it in front of her closet mirror, and then took it off.

She heard the front door open and the slap of the screen door. She heard her father call out, "*Estoy aquí.* I'm home!" She heard her father's tired feet trudge to the kitchen, where the faucet came on with a whine. She knew he was drinking a glass of cool water.

That night, over a dinner of *chile verde*, *sopa*, and *frijoles*, Miata asked her father, "Papi, you ever run for something?"

Miata's father smiled. *"Pues*, when I was your age, I used to run from Juan Delgado, a bad dude I knew."

"Nah, Dad, I mean did you ever run for office? Like at school?" Miata scraped a tortilla across her plate, gathering up the juices of the *chile verde*. She looked up at her father, waiting for his answer. She hoped that he would be able to give her some advice.

"You mean like a treasurer or something?"

"Yeah," Miata said brightly, both elbows propped on the table.

Her father thought hard, his cheeks bulging and slowly rolling with food. He swallowed and cleared his throat. "I used to be cocaptain of the Wrestling Club."

"The Wrestling Club," Miata repeated in a near whisper. This was not what she had expected to hear. She had hoped to hear that her ancestors had held a long list of important positions in the government—governor of Jalisco, mayor of Guadalajara, or even postmaster of the littlest of little Mexican *pueblos*—that she could be proud of. But she caught herself. She suspected she was being disloyal to her family, which had had an ordinary past. Miata smiled at her father and listened.

"Yeah, I used to wrestle for the Boys Club. They elected me because Grampa was the only one with a truck. He used to fit us in the back and drive us places." He reflected on his past and crowed, "Yeah, we were bad. Like bad bad."

"You mean no good?" Joey piped up.

"*¡Simón!*" Their father smiled. "But we had some tough-looking uniforms."

"Well, Dad, that's not exactly the same thing. You know, I meant like when people vote for you." Miata explained that she was running for school president.

"No, I can't say that I ever did that." Her father drank from his water glass and said to his wife, "*Ay*, this food is the best." Then he turned back to Miata and said, "Sweetie, I would vote for you for president any day." He got up, scraping the chair against the floor. He went into the kitchen to help himself to seconds.

When he came back to the table, Joey said, "Dad, after dinner I'm going to show you something really scary."

Miata looked at her little brother. It's cute that he doesn't give up, she thought.

"What is it?" her father asked Joey.

"It might give you nightmares," Joey warned.

"I can take it, champ."

"It might make you throw up," Joey warned a second time. He let out a soft burp and giggled.

"¡Ay!" their mother scolded. "Don't talk like that at the dinner table."

"Yeah," Joey's father said, his face close to the plate. "Save it for when you and me do the dishes." He gave his son a wink and scraped his plate clean.

After dinner, Miata returned to her bedroom and completed her reading assignment. Afterward she brought out her best stationery, the one decorated with a cat peeking out of a basket. She decided to write to the president of the United States for advice. Using a purple pen, she wrote:

Dear Mr. President,
I'm writing for your advice because you
have done the impossible. You have
become the president of our country.
Congratulations! I want to become
president of my school. I'm hoping to improve the conditions
there. My running mate is Ana,
my best friend. Anyhow, we only
got two weeks. Could you tell us
something about winning? We
need help.

Sincerely,
Miata Ramirez

P.S. My dad and mom didn't vote
for you but I hope that's OK and
it didn't hurt your feelings.

Miata reread the letter, her lips moving over
each word. She thought it sounded honest. She ad-
dressed an envelope, licked a stamp, and put the
letter in her backpack.

That night she dreamed about galloping on a racehorse. In her dream, she took sharp corners and bit down hard on her teeth. She woke up, rested. She thought the dream meant something important. She jumped out of bed, whinnied like a horse, and clopped off to the bathroom to wash up for the day.

CHAPTER 3

Miata scanned the audience sitting on the floor in the multipurpose room, which was still decorated with banners for the sixteenth of September, Mexican Independence Day. The heads of the fifth-graders wagged like apples on a branch. Miata was nervous about the debate. But this was her big chance to tell the students why they should vote for her and not for Rudy.

Miata looked at Rudy sitting next to her. She could see that he was chewing gum, which was against school rules. He was smacking his lips and waving to the boys in the audience.

Blowing a bubble, Rudy turned to Miata. The

bubble grew as large as a fist and popped like a fist in a baseball glove. He laughed and asked, "You want some gum?"

"No, it's against school rules," Miata said. "I'm not going to get in trouble just before elections."

"Oh yeah, that's right," Rudy said. He swallowed the bubble gum and opened his mouth like an alligator's. His throat blared "Ahhhhhhhhh." He closed his mouth and said, "See, it's all gone."

"That's ugly, Rudy." Miata grimaced.

Rudy shrugged his shoulders. He turned his attention to the audience. Someone was yelling at Rudy to ask if he wanted to exchange his sandwich for a burrito during lunch. Rudy gave him a thumbs-up response.

Miata's nervous knees shivered, and the lines on her palms ran with sticky sweat. She looked down at the five MIATA AND ANA badges on the front of her blouse. Earlier they had seemed so neat, but now they just got in her way.

"People—fifth-graders—let's settle down," Mrs. Castillo, the vice principal, yelled above the noise.

She repeated her command and gradually the bob-bing heads stopped moving.

"Yeah, let's knock it off," Rudy yelled, getting to his feet. His gaze locked on two boys who were pushing each other. "Carlos, leave Jaime alone. Save it for the playground."

Carlos stopped shoving his friend and sat up as straight as an angel, which he was not.

"That's better," Rudy said. He then returned to his seat.

"Thank you, Rudy," Mrs. Castillo said.

"No problem," he said.

Mrs. Castillo turned to Miata and, with a smile, said sweetly, "We're going to hear from Miata first. She's in room six. Let's hear what she has to say."

There was light applause as Miata rose from her chair and approached the podium. She climbed onto a box that was set there for her. She adjusted the microphone.

"Good morning," Miata said.

"It's almost afternoon," Carlos yelled.

Miata looked at the clock on the wall and then at Carlos. She decided to ignore him. She contin-ued with a bright chime in her voice. "I'm seeking your votes next Tuesday. I want to be your president."

"President of the United States?" Carlos yelled through the funnel of his hands.

With that, Mrs. Castillo, now stern faced, shook a finger at him. He returned to sitting as straight as an angel.

Miata breathed in as she gathered strength. She inflated her lungs and boomed, "If elected, I plan to beautify the school grounds. I want to get rid of all that *cholo* graffiti and put some flowers in by our fifth-grade rooms."

Some of the students, mostly girls, applauded.

"I'm sure you're tired of a *cochino*-looking school," Miata boomed even louder.

There was more applause, but not enough to make Miata confident. She eyed Ana in the audience. Ana hadn't clapped that hard. Miata clicked her tongue and thought, Come on, Ana, let's get with it.

"Those are good ideas," Ana remarked, not too bravely. She looked around the audience. No one was applauding.

Miata paused, somewhat shaken. She had practiced with Ana on the school grounds, but now behind the podium the words didn't seem as powerful.

"I plan to get parents involved," Miata continued. "I want them to help with the cleanup."

Only one student applauded. It was Carlos. He was applauding as hard as rain on a car roof. He wouldn't stop until Mrs. Castillo beckoned him with a finger. He was being called out of the room. He rose to his feet and said, "I'll vote for you, Miata. You're nicer." Then, looking at Rudy, Carlos stepped over his classmates sitting on the floor. "Nah, I better vote for Rudy. I owe him a quarter." He was prodded from the multipurpose room toward the principal's office.

"Just think," Miata said, her voice weak. She was losing her confidence. "We can put some really nice azaleas and pansies outside our windows. The walls will be all clean, not like they are now." She looked at her scribbled notes, then up toward the audience. "It'll be work, but we can do it."

The audience scrunched up their faces.

"And I have plans for a school trip," Miata

countered quickly, sensing that she was losing her listeners. "And I have a fund-raising idea for how we can get computers with CD-ROMs."

The audience yawned. Two posters that said VOTE FOR MIATA AND ANA sank down.

"I have a question," a boy said, his hand as tall as a spear.

"Yes."

"Are we gonna get paid to work?" His face was lit with a grin. He knew he was being silly.

"No, we're not getting paid. It's for our school."

The students muttered but applauded lightly. A few of the posters went up again in a rattle but quickly sank down.

"Please think of me when you vote on Tuesday," Miata said. Her voice was now as faint as a baby bird's chirp.

She sat down, exhausted. She wanted to shake her head in defeat but knew that she had to sit up bravely. She waved at the audience, but only a few students waved back. Not one of them was a boy.

Then Rudy stood up. He approached the podium and leaped onto the box.

"Hey, I like this," he laughed. As he held on to

the podium, he wobbled the box and said, "It's like a skateboard!"

The audience laughed. From where she sat, Miata could see that more than one boy was chewing bubble gum.

Rudy then became serious. He looked at Miata and said, "She's got some ideas. Miata would make a good prez, but I think I would make a truly great one."

The audience laughed.

"And you know why?" Rudy asked.

"Why?" some of the boys in the audience repeated.

Rudy turned a cupped ear to the audience. "I can't hear you."

"Why?" yelled a mixed group of boys and girls.

"Still can't hear you." Rudy smiled.

"*Why?*" the entire audience yelled.

Rudy nodded his head, smiling. He had their attention. "It's because . . . I'm going to work to get us more recess time."

The audience applauded and chanted, "More recess! More recess! More recess!"

"Yeah, *gente*! Instead of just fifteen minutes, I'm

going to ask the principal for twenty—at least! Maybe even a half hour, homeboys!"

"Why not an hour?" someone yelled from the audience.

"We can't push our luck, dude," Rudy responded.

Miata wanted to cover her face. It was obvious that the audience was siding with Rudy.

Rudy raised his hands and asked for silence.

"Plus," he continued as he slowly scanned the audience. "Plus I'm going to ask for Ice Cream Day every day. Not just on Fridays."

The audience roared as Rudy wobbled the box and then jumped off. He returned to his seat, pushing a fresh piece of bubble gum into his mouth.

"You got good ideas," Rudy said with confidence. "Good luck. *Buena suerte.*" He extended a hand.

"Yeah, thanks. I'll need it," Miata said in a whisper as she stood up and shook Rudy's hand, which was as cool as a lizard's. "Good luck to you, too, Rudy."

After the debate, the students returned to their classrooms. Miata tried to put on a good face. Most

of the girls knew that Rudy was a joker. They knew he could never get that extra five minutes of recess or Ice Cream Day five days a week. But the boys might believe him. Miata needed a new strategy.

After school, she returned home and started her homework behind the closed door of her bedroom. But her mind stalled. She kept looking at the photo of herself taken in Mexico when she was five years old. She was on a pony. Her smile was big and her eyes lit with happiness.

"That was fun," she whispered as she remembered how her Uncle Jorge led her around the yard. At the time she had thought that she was going really fast, but now she knew that it must have been slower than a trot.

Miata put down her homework and looked in her scrapbook at her dad's family in Mexico—her grandparents and uncles and aunts. They all lived north of Guadalajara, on a *rancho.*

Then, toward dark, she heard her father come home. She heard the screen door slam and his heavy trudge to the kitchen. She heard the groan of the faucet and then her father calling, "Miata! *¡Ven acá!*"

Miata let the pencil roll from her hand. She was tired of doing her math problems.

"*¡Sí!*" Miata yelled as she scooted back her chair. She hurried into the living room. "What's up, Papi?"

"I found something at work."

"What?"

"A most unusual thing."

"What is it? Tell me."

He was holding a small white box in his hand.

"It scared me when I found it." Her father's face was dark with worry and dust from his long hours at work.

Miata furrowed her brow. She was curious.

Slowly her father lifted the lid from the box. Miata peeked in, standing on her tiptoes. In it stood an adult index finger that was as gnarled as a root. She eyed her father and clicked her tongue.

"Where do you think it came from, *mi'ja*?" her father asked seriously. He petted the finger with his free hand.

"From your left hand, Papi," Miata answered, hands on her hips. "That's where it came from."

A sudden smile brightened his face. He wiggled the finger in the box and screamed, "*Ay*, it's coming alive. I better put it down the garbage disposal." He ran into the kitchen laughing, and Miata followed her father. But he only got himself another glass of water.

"Dad?" Miata asked, taking his large work-stained hand into hers.

"Yeah, *mi'ja*." He wiped his mouth with the back of his free hand.

"Do you think I should run for office?" She hesitated and then continued. "I mean, I'm not as popular as Rudy or his friend Alex."

"Well, popularity is one thing, but service is another. *¿Entiendes?*"

Miata shook her head. She was confused.

"I mean, it's OK to have a lot of people who like you, but it's far better to help people, to get things done." He gave her a light hug. "Don't worry. Just go for it. If it doesn't happen, *pues*, you can still do good."

Miata liked that. She had plans for the school, and they were good ones. She figured that she could still do them without being president.

Nearly skipping, she returned to her bedroom and got to work on her math, the numbers tumbling from her mind like cereal. Dad is pretty neat, she thought as she sharpened her pencil, which was chewed along its length. The teeth marks were a reminder of how hungry she was to study and to make her family proud.

"Miata!" her mother called from the living room. *"Una llamada."*

She put down her pencil, just as she was getting into the swing of her math problems. She nearly galloped to the living room and picked up the telephone. "Yes?"

"If I could, I'd vote for Rudy. He's cute," a girl teased in a singsong voice.

"Who is this?"

There was giggling, but no one spoke. Miata was getting a crank call.

"Go ahead and laugh," Miata growled. Miata laughed back, but there was no joy.

The laughing continued, and still no one spoke.

Miata kept her ear to the telephone, hoping to pick up the sound of a voice, a blaring radio, a television program—clues that might identify the caller.

"Who is this?" Miata repeated.

"Who is this?" the person mimicked.

"You're sick," Miata yelled.

The telephone clicked and went dead just as Miata began to threaten to call the police.

Miata slowly put the telephone back into its cradle. She had been so happy after her father's wise words, and now this call left her feeling annoyed at some anonymous person from school.

CHAPTER
4

Miata decided to ignore the phone call and to tell neither her parents nor Ana about it. She decided to push ahead, though she intended to remember that laugh.

In the garage, Miata pushed some flower seeds into the moist earth cupped in egg cartons. She pushed them in gently, sprinkled them with the blessing of water, and cooed, "Grow, my little friends. *¡Apúrense!* Hurry up!" In two weeks, she hoped, they would be as tall as pencils and ready to plant around the school grounds. Miata's mother had told her that it was the wrong time to grow flowers, but Miata stuck with her promise to beautify their drab school. She couldn't go back on her promise.

She turned her attention to an azalea cutting stuffed in a milk carton. A few of its leaves had parachuted from the dark branches. Some of the other leaves were as pale as weak tea.

"Don't die," she yelled at the bush. Then she softened her heart as she bent down and begged the plant to grow up and be pretty.

Two more leaves fell from the branches.

Miata planned to take the azalea to school and plant it near room 6. In her mind, she could see it growing healthy and green and so bright you would need sunglasses to admire it. She pictured the flowers she had seen floating on the lake of Xochimilco in Mexico. That's what I'll do, she thought. I'll turn our school into a lake of beautiful flowers.

She slapped dirt from her palms, snapped off the light, and left the garage. It was a cool night. A blade of clouds cut across the dark sky, and the wind rustled the fall leaves of their sycamore. Miata stood there in the silence, smiling because the girls at school had said they would vote for her and Ana. They agreed that the boys fooled around too much to lead the school. Also, their spelling was poor, and their math skills were just a little better than two plus two.

She went back inside the house, confident that she and Ana would win.

"Mom," Miata yelled, wiping her feet on the mat. "You ready?"

Her mother was in the kitchen, reading a magazine. She answered without looking up, "OK, mi'ja. But isn't Ana coming?"

Just then the doorbell rang, sending an echo resounding throughout the house. Miata, hurrying to the door, skipped from the kitchen to the living room. Her father and brother were playing checkers on the rug. She could see that Joey was winning, his red checkers quickly piling up. But she knew that her dad was letting him win. When she was Joey's age—eight years old—she used to play checkers with her dad and win big time. Now that she was ten, almost eleven, she knew that her dad had been playing dumb.

"You winning?" Miata asked as she hurried to the front door.

"Yeah, but Dad's got two of mine," Joey said, not looking up.

Miata let Ana in, and the two girls hurried to the kitchen.

"Hello, Ana," Miata's mother said as she rose from her chair and closed her magazine. "Are you sure your mommy said it's OK to perm your hair?"

Miata and Ana had talked earlier about changing their image. They figured that the best way to get votes was to look different. And at their age, they also figured, the only part of them they could change was their hair. They decided to get perms.

"Yes, Mrs. Ramirez," Ana answered shyly.

Mrs. Ramirez turned Ana around and around, pulling softly at her long hair. "You have pretty hair, *mi'ja*."

"Thank you," Ana answered simply. "Will it hurt?"

Mrs. Ramirez smiled and said, "No, the perm won't hurt, Ana."

Ana still looked worried. She wasn't very daring and was as shy as a turtle backing into its shell. It had surprised everyone when she became Miata's running mate. Now she was getting her hair stylishly permed.

"You girls are going to look pretty," Mrs. Ramirez said. "*Ándenle.* Let's go to the bathroom."

The three of them hurried to the bathroom, where Mrs. Ramirez wrapped their shoulders with old towels. She twisted red plastic curlers into Ana's hair and then blue ones into Miata's hair. She mixed the perm lotion and squirted it into each curl. Then she fit a plastic cap over the curls, locking in the fumes.

"Mom," Miata asked as she sat on the edge of the bathtub, "you ever have a perm?"

Mrs. Ramirez ran a hand through her hair, which was as glossy and black as new asphalt. "No, *mi'ja.* But I did wear it short for a while."

"How short?"

Mrs. Ramirez indicated the length with her thumb and index finger.

"That was pretty short, Mom," Miata cried.

Her mom added, "And it was purple."

"Purple!" both girls screamed.

"Yeah, it was when I was at City College. That was the style."

"Wow, Mrs. Ramirez," Ana said. "You were radical!"

After Mrs. Ramirez left the bathroom, Miata and Ana began to talk about the worst movie they had ever seen. For Miata, it was *Blockheads*, a science fiction movie about people from outer space. Their heads were shaped like huge concrete blocks. For Ana, the worst movie had been made by her cousin Eddie, a college student. He had shown it at Thanksgiving the year before, and as far as she could tell, it was about nothing. It was just about a man who walked around pushing a shopping cart.

After a while, Miata looked at herself in the mirror. Pretty weird, she thought. She sprayed some of her mom's perfume on her wrists and rubbed them together. Ana did the same and then sneezed from the smell.

Twenty minutes later, Mrs. Ramirez returned to the bathroom.

"How are you girls?" she asked as she poked at Ana's plastic cap.

"Fine," they both answered.

Humming, Mrs. Ramirez peeled off their caps. Then she began to unwrap the rows of plastic curlers from Miata's hair. They popped off, one by one.

"What happened?" Mrs. Ramirez said, mildly shocked. "They seem crazy." She plucked a curl with her finger.

Miata looked in the mirror, big eyed. The perm was much too wavy.

"Mom!" Miata cried. "What did you do?"

"I don't know, *mi'ja*," Mrs. Ramirez answered. She picked up the box and read the directions again, her mouth silently forming each word. She shook her head and said, "Oh, no! I kind of messed up. I was supposed to add three-quarters water."

She undid the curls from Ana's hair, and the results were the same—hair that was as puffy as cotton candy and just as sticky.

"*Es feo*," Miata growled as she faced her mother. "It's so ugly."

"No, it's pretty," Mrs. Ramirez countered. "It's

46

got a lot of body. It'll look even better when it's not wet."

The girls stared at the mirror. Their new hairdos looked like the wigs they had worn when they went trick-or-treating as witches in the first grade.

"Maybe you should shampoo it right away and wash out some of the bounce," Mrs. Ramirez suggested.

Ana turned to Miata, and Miata, hands on hips, turned to her mother as Mrs. Ramirez tiptoed from the bathroom. Both girls felt like crying, but they knew it would do no good. They washed their new hairdos, but the stubborn waves remained.

"What are we going to do?" Ana asked as she patted the top of her head.

"Get out of town?" Miata suggested, fiddling with the frizz around her ears.

Miata's mother returned and quieted the girls down. She reminded them that perms don't last forever. Then she added that they both looked darling. Neither of them believed her.

The next day Miata and Ana met early at the

school gate, both wearing baseball caps down to their ears. They glanced nervously about.

"We look dumb," Miata lamented. She was carrying the azalea, which was more a stick than an actual plant. Only a few leaves clung to the branches.

Ana took off her cap and complained, "I can't wear this thing."

Miata removed her cap as well. She stuffed the cap in her backpack and pulled out a fistful of fliers. As the students arrived at school, the girls handed out fliers that read VOTE FOR THE BEST.

The students took the fliers, all of them repeatedly asking, "What happened to your hair?"

Miata then cocked her head and whispered out of the side of her mouth, "Here comes you know who."

Rudy was on the handlebars of Alex's wobbling bike. He was eating a pig-shaped cookie. With his eyes closed and savoring the taste, Rudy bit its corkscrew of a tail.

When Rudy spotted the girls, he waved with his free hand, upsetting the balance of the bike. Alex lost control, they started to topple over, and the bike slammed against the curb. The pig cookie flew from Rudy's hand. It broke into crumbs as the front tire climbed over its stomach.

"Hey, man," Rudy squealed. "You killed the cookie."

Alex was on his knees, a new skid mark on his jeans. He looked up, wincing in pain, and noticed Miata's hair.

"What happened, girl?" Alex asked as he rose to his feet.

"Nothing," Miata said.

Rudy's mouth gaped open like a sack. He touched his own hair and remarked, "*Híjole*, Miata, that's a real different hairdo."

Rudy circled Miata, a finger on his chin, as he sized her up. He finally flopped his arms at his side and concluded, "Yeah, it looks good."

Miata ignored this compliment and handed him a flier.

Rudy took it and mumbled, "Vote for the Best."

"Umm, catchy," Alex said. "Look at ours."

Rudy pushed his hand into his own backpack and brought out their flier, which read HOMIES FOR

50

MORE RECESS AND ICE CREAM/GET DOWN, *GENTE*, AND VOTE FOR A REAL MEAN TEAM. From his stack, he peeled off one for Miata and one for Ana.

Miata examined the flier and shoved it into her pocket. "How can you make these promises?" she asked.

"Easy," Rudy sang. "All you gotta do is just say things people might like to hear. Like the president."

"You're not the president," Ana said.

"No," Rudy said as he looked down at the azalea. "I just talk like him." He raised a hand slowly, pointed and said, "*¡Chihuahua!* What's that? A sick tree?"

"Yeah, homes," Alex remarked. "Looks like it needs some vitamins or something."

"It's an azalea," Miata said. "It's the start of our Beautification Program."

Rudy looked at Alex and the two mouthed, "Beautification Program?"

"That's right," Ana said, moving closer to Miata.

After Rudy and Alex walked away, Miata pulled the boys' flier out of her pocket. She reread it, crumpled it, tossed it in the air, and booted it with her sneaker as Ana giggled. But Miata hated littering and picked it up again.

"Come on," Miata said when she heard the bell ring. The girls entered the school with a whirlwind of curls bouncing on their heads.

CHAPTER
5

During morning recess, Miata and Ana planted the azalea near the door to their classroom. They fit the plant snugly into its hole and sprinkled water on it, using a coffee can.

"There," Miata said, determined to make her school beautiful. She patted the dirt with the flat of her palms and stood up, smiling.

A crowd of students, mostly girls, looked on. They stared at the scraggly plant and then at Miata's hairdo. Finally one of them asked, "Miata, how come you and Ana got your hair like that? Are you in a gang?"

"No, we're not in a gang," Miata said. "My

mom just used too much perm solution on our hair."

Ana added, "Even moms can make mistakes."

A wind whipped up and brushed off a few more leaves from the azalea.

"Are you really going to make our school pretty?" a girl asked.

"Yes, we are," Miata said. She could see that she finally had their attention. She began to explain her plan. She would get parents to help the students paint over the graffiti, fix the broken swings, wax the auditorium floor, and adjust the sprinklers so that they didn't shoot straight up in the air. She even promised better cafeteria food.

Two girls yawned, and one remarked, "Sounds like a lot of work. I think I'll vote for Rudy and Alex."

"You don't want to do that," Miata said. "Come on. Girls gotta stick together."

"Yeah," Ana chimed in. "Like *frijoles* and tortillas."

"Like guacamole and chips," Miata sang.

"Like soda and sunflower seeds," Ana yelled, and danced.

"Like Rudy and Alex," Rudy sang above them all. The boys were sitting in the sycamore tree that stood near the classroom. Their faces were greasy from eating barbecue potato chips. Rudy licked his orange-tinted fingers, held up his bag of chips, and mumbled, "You want some, Miata?"

Miata shaded her eyes and looked at the boys, sitting side by side on a gnarly limb. When the recess bell rang, the crowd dispersed toward the classrooms, and Rudy and Alex dropped like huge fruit from the tree. At the impact, air coughed from their bellies. Laughing, they got up from their knees and brushed grass off themselves.

"Those boys," Miata mumbled to Ana as they hurried to their class, where, for a change, they didn't have to open their books. A magician, a man who reportedly owned a chicken that could play the piano, had been invited to perform for the school. A brilliant situation, Miata thought. She could pester her friends to vote for her and Ana.

"Let's file in quietly. No talking!" Mrs. Diaz warned. She monitored the students, now and then pulling a bad kid from the line. She told Miata to stop handing out fliers, and she did.

The students settled on the floor of the multipurpose room. They sat cross-legged and stared at the magician, a short man with a goatee. He was wearing black pants with a black T-shirt. Rings sparkled on his chubby fingers like knives.

"We're in for a special treat," Mr. Rios roared as he stood in front of the audience. He tried to look jolly, though most of the kids knew him as a tough cookie. "Abracadabra! Let me present to you a former street magician from Mexico City, Señor Gomez the Magnificent."

Señor Gomez the Magnificent smiled as he bowed deeply to the applause. He bowed again and asked for quiet. He wet his lips. His front teeth were edged with gold. Each of his wrists was bluish black with tattoos of chains.

"He looks like my *tío* Arturo," Miata whispered in Ana's ears.

"*Buenas tardes*," Señor Gomez growled.

"*Buenas tardes*," the students replied. They were all happy to be doing something other than schoolwork.

As he gazed around the audience, the magician washed his hands with the air and—presto—a nickel appeared. He flipped the coin into the air, and it came down as a dime. He flipped the dime into the air, and it came down as a quarter.

"I'm getting rich, *muchachos.*" He smiled.

He flipped the quarter, and it came down as a silver dollar. He tossed the silver dollar up, and it came down as a rose. He sniffed it and then handed it to Mrs. Diaz, who smiled and thanked him.

The audience clapped, and the magician smiled again, showing his gold teeth.

"*Mira,*" he announced. "Cool, clear *agua.*" He took a tiny, bird-sized sip from his silver cup and poured the remaining water into a glass. As he did, the clear water changed to blue. He then poured the blue water into another glass. The water became as red as an icy strawberry Popsicle.

"I saw that before," a boy in the audience said.

"*Sí, muchacho,*" the magician said, his teeth winking gold. He reached for the boy's ear and brought out a *cochino* bug.

"You better wash your ears, *joven.*" Señor Gomez laughed and then froze, his eyes big. He looked down at his arm. A snake, as thin as a yellow pencil, slithered from the sleeve of his T-shirt. The snake's tongue flared in and out as the animal wrapped its body around Señor Gomez's neck. Pretending to be choking, Señor Gomez bulged out his eyes and let his tongue dangle from his mouth.

"*Qué feo*," Ana said, looking away.

"Yeah," Miata agreed. She touched her throat. She wondered how it felt to have a snake coiled around your throat. She gulped and breathed in deeply.

"Do you know what this little fellow's name is?" Señor Gomez asked as he let the snake coil around his arm, which itself was coiled with a snake tattoo. "*Se llama* Bopper."

Ana gasped and grabbed Miata's hand. She didn't like snakes, frogs, toads, lizards, or any other small creatures without fur. Animal skin scared her, and even the thought of shoving a baseball glove on her hand gave her a creepy feeling. She knew that the glove had once been the living skin of a cow.

Without much thought, Miata took the hand of the person sitting next to her.

"There, there," a voice said as Miata felt someone patting her hand.

Miata turned and saw that Rudy was sitting next to her, having scooted up from the middle row to be near the front. She looked down at Rudy's hand, which was resting on top of hers. Startled, she pulled her hand away and stared at Rudy. Miata was embarrassed.

"Oh," she mumbled. "Sorry. I didn't know I was holding your hand."

"No problem, girl. It was fun." Rudy grinned.

Miata blushed but looked up when everyone started screaming. Her eyes locked on Bopper the snake, which was slowly disappearing down Señor Gomez the Magnificent's throat. She watched in horror as it descended inch by inch.

"*¡Asco!*" Miata was shocked at the thought of someone eating a live snake.

There was more screaming. The snake appeared, mouth agape, slithering from Señor Gomez's ear. He yanked it out of his ear and rolled it between his palms like a pencil. He rolled it until the snake disappeared and then held out the palms of his hands to show the audience. The snake was gone. When Señor Gomez bowed, the audience began to clap.

"*Y ahora*, I need a volunteer. Someone who is brave, *valiente*, good-looking, smart, *y chico*."

Rudy immediately stood up and said, "Señor, you must be talking about me." A shy glow beamed from his cheeks as he looked down at his tennis shoes. "How can I help you?"

"*Bueno*," Señor Gomez said as he studied Rudy. He turned him around, lifted him up to see how heavy he was, and patted his head. "An excellent candidate to . . ." He turned and smiled at the audience. He rubbed his hands together and lifted one eyebrow, a look of pretend evilness coloring his face. "An excellent candidate to saw in half!"

Rudy looked at Señor Gomez and tottered on the heels of his tennis shoes. His mouth fell open. "Señor, I'm already short. If you cut me in half, I'll have to go back to third grade."

"*¡No te preocupes!*" Señor Gomez argued. "Don't worry, *joven*. I'll put you back together with some string and tape."

The fourth- and fifth-graders stretched their

necks when Señor Gomez wheeled in a squeaky cart carrying a long, painted box. A handsaw was pressed in his armpit.

"Young man," Señor Gomez said, "I want you to climb in and take a little siesta." He removed the lid and then lifted Rudy and placed him in the box.

Rudy shrugged his shoulders, pretending not to be scared, and said to the audience, "I guess I'll go to bed." He lay down and scooted into a comfortable position. His head stuck out at one end of the box, and his feet stuck out at the other.

"Close your eyes," Señor Gomez said as he fit the lid onto the box and raised his saw.

"See you later, Rudy," a boy in the audience screamed. "¡Adiós! Nice to know you."

"¡Adiós!" Rudy yelled. To Alex, his best friend, he said, "You can have my G.I. Joes."

"Now just relax, young man," Señor Gomez said. He bent the saw and flicked it with his finger. A twangy hum rose from the metal blade.

He worked the saw into a slot in the middle of the box. He started sawing back and forth, back and forth, while Rudy lay motionless and staring at the audience. Clowning around, Señor Gomez stopped to wipe his brow and made his chest puff up and down as if he were exhausted.

"How do you feel?" Señor Gomez asked Rudy.

"Fine," Rudy said. "Except my nose itches."

Señor Gomez scratched Rudy's nose for him and then went around and scratched the bottoms of his sneakers. He turned to the audience and hollered through the funnel of his big hands, "I need a volunteer—a girl who is also brave, smart, *guapa*, and a leader in the school."

Miata sprang to her feet. She figured he was referring to her. She stepped between her classmates and skipped to the front.

"What do you want me to do?"

"Saw your friend in half—cut him up like you might cut an enchilada." Señor Gomez pointed to the saw.

"No, Miata," Rudy whined. "Don't saw me in half! I just had lunch." Rudy wiggled his tennis shoes and knocked about in the box.

"Won't it hurt Rudy?" Miata asked Señor Gomez, her face scrunched up.

"Nah. Not a young man like this."

"Are you sure?"

"*Simón.* Go for it, *muchacha!*"

Miata breathed in deeply as she swung around and faced the box. Rudy pretended to be scared. "Come on, Miata. Don't do it," he begged. "We're friends."

"Are we?"

"Yeah. In fact, I'll give you my Barry Bonds baseball."

"No thanks. It got me in trouble." Miata gripped the handle of the saw and began to work it slowly back and forth, back and forth. A light sweat shone on her forehead as the action of the saw picked up.

"Does it hurt?" Miata asked, nearly out of breath but still sawing away.

"Only when I laugh," Rudy said. He laughed and then made a sad face like a circus clown who has tripped over his own shoes.

Miata had to smile at Rudy. The saw worked through the box and came out through the bottom. For a moment she thought she had actually cut Rudy in half because he had closed his eyes, pretending to be dead.

"Are you dead?" Miata asked.

"I think so," Rudy said, eyes closed. He then smiled and laughed so hard that his bubble gum shot from his mouth and bounced off Miata's forehead.

"*¡Cochino!*" Miata laughed, touching her forehead. "You know you're not supposed to be chewing gum!"

Miata thought of throwing the gum at Rudy's forehead, but she remembered where she was, in front of the fourth- and fifth-graders and the sixty or so voters. She turned and bowed to the audience and handed the saw to the magician.

"*Mira,*" Señor Gomez called out as he pushed the box back together. "What a strong young man!"

Rudy climbed out of the box, patted his belly, and bowed to the applause. Then, hamming it up, he walked on his knees, only half the boy he once was, and sang "Vote for me, vote for me and my big friend Alex!"

The classmates applauded, and over the applause Miata heard a laugh that was as obnoxious as the one on the telephone. The laughter was like the *quack-quack* of a duck. She scanned the audience. The students all seemed to have their mouths open, the winds of laughter filling the multipurpose room.

Where is she? Miata thought. Her eyes narrowed into slits as she looked about.

"Let's go," Mrs. Diaz said. "No pushing."

As the noisy students filed from the room and back to their classes, Miata cracked her knuckles. She promised herself that she would find that girl.

CHAPTER 6

Señor Gomez the Magnificent had, in fact, been magnificent. Rudy had been brilliantly sawed in half and then put back together. The week had been exciting. Now, Friday morning, Miata hopped onto the school bus, joining her class-mates, who were squawking like parrots. She found a torn, graffiti-inked seat near the middle, where Ana sat nibbling on an animal cracker—a hippo slowly being chewed to a paste. How appro-priate, as they were off on a field trip to the zoo.

"Here, you want some?" Ana asked. She handed Miata a lion cracker with one of its paws gone.

Miata thanked her friend and put the lion to sleep on the bed of her pink tongue. Instead of chewing it, she let it rest there, like a host at Communion.

The bus pulled from the parking lot, the heads of the fifth-graders bouncing. The bus lurched and finally picked up speed. They bounced and swayed thirty miles to the Fresno Zoo. They passed acres and acres of vineyards, orange groves, plum and nectarine orchards, and a few dairies where black-and-white cows ate from long troughs.

"¡Fuchi!" Miata complained, pinching her nose with her fingers.

After nearly an hour's drive, they pulled into the parking lot of the zoo, got off the bus, and enjoyed a snack. The girls sat with the girls, and the boys sat with the boys. They ate quickly, and then the boys started to fool with the sprinklers, squirting each other, until Mrs. Diaz and two parents told them to knock it off.

"We're trying to fix them," Rudy explained. He was drenched, his hair spiky and the collar of his T-shirt pulled down to his ribs.

Mrs. Diaz threatened to leave him on the bus if

he didn't behave, and this was enough to make Rudy calm down.

"We're going to win," Miata said as she gobbled an apple slice. She inhaled her juice until the box collapsed. "Boys can't behave like elected officials."

The students were herded through the turnstile and immediately came upon a camel, which was slowly chewing a mouthful of straw. Its eyes were a dark coffee color and its hide a woolly brown. A crown of flies buzzed around its head. Some of the flies broke away and started to circle the students.

"I hate flies," Miata told Ana, who nodded her head in agreement. Ana told her friend how she once had gotten some 7-Up and one of the ice cubes had had a fly in it.

"*¡Asco!*" Miata cried.

"But it wasn't a real fly," Ana said. "It was one of those plastic cubes that look real. It was a stupid joke from my cousin José."

The students then moved to a caged hyena, which was pacing back and forth. It appeared to be muttering to itself, almost talking. Miata felt sorry for the animal. It seemed so bored.

In a nearby cage, an arctic fox sat near its water trough. Its nose was as black as an olive.

"I thought foxes were bigger," Miata said as she shoved her way between two boys.

"Nah, they're really small. They're so cute," Ana said, tiptoeing and trying to see.

A voice asked, "Are you talking about us?"

Miata turned her head and saw that she was standing between Rudy and Alex. Rudy snapped his fingers and cooed, "Come on, doggy. Come on! Roll over for Little Rudy!" The fox yawned and swept some leaves with a whisk of its tail.

"Rudy, he's not a dog! He's a fox!" Miata read the description of the fox, which said, in Latin, *Alopex lagopus.*

Rudy read the description, nodded his head, and said, "That's a cool name he's got!"

Miata pushed herself away from the iron rail that circled the cage. She left to look at the giraffe, which was as tall as a banana tree and just as slim.

Miata stared at the animal, amazed by its height. She remembered that when she was four, she had gotten a stuffed toy giraffe from Tía Rosa for Christmas. She loved that stuffed animal. Wherever she went, even to church, she cuddled its little body. Then, one day, her mother threw it into the washing machine. Miata cried when she saw Giraffey bobbing among the soapy white things— T-shirts, socks, and underwear. Later her mother hung it by its ears on the clothesline. This made Miata cry even more.

"I got a cousin that's almost as tall as that giraffe," Rudy boasted as he gripped the rail next to Miata.

"Oh sure, Rudy," Miata teased.

"Yeah, girl, he's really tall. He's the tallest *raza* in all the world, girl."

"*¡Simón!* I saw the dude, too," Alex agreed, hitching up his pants. He looked skyward, as if he were staring at clouds. "You could hardly see his eyes, he was way, way up there."

"Right," Miata said in disbelief. But, unable to help herself, she looked up and followed Alex's gaze. She felt stupid.

Rudy explained that his cousin was as tall as a short giraffe, not a regular giraffe. He said the cousin had almost played for the NBA but had joined the army instead.

Ana rolled her eyes and said, "Yeah, sure. A short giraffe."

Miata pushed away from the guardrail. Ana followed, along with some other girls.

They admired the shaggy herd of bison, the rhinoceros, the flat-footed ostrich, an alligator that was yawning, and a pair of zebras, which reminded Miata of the bedsheets she had once slept on—black-and-white stripes. The students traveled to Monkey Island, where chimps with orange teeth begged for handouts. The sign said DON'T FEED THE ANIMALS.

"But they look so cute," Ana said, touching her heart. She had a speckled banana in her backpack. She thought of giving it to the chimps but knew that it was against the rules.

"I wish I could swing like that," Miata sighed, admiring a chimpanzee. He was hanging on to a tree limb with only his thumb and index finger. With his free hand, he was holding a carrot like a baton. "He's pretty cool."

From Monkey Island they ventured into a dank-smelling cave full of toads. The animals were like blobs, warted and hideous as they breathed in and out. There were lizards and toads, and reptiles that looked as ancient as the first living things of this world.

"Snakes!" Miata pointed to the rattler coiled behind greasy, finger-stained glass. She tapped on the glass, but the snake didn't move.

"You like it?" a voice said overhead.

At first she thought it was Rudy again, but the voice was deep. When Miata turned and looked up, she peered into a familiar face. The face smiled, revealing teeth edged with gold.

"Señor Gomez!" Miata yelled.

The classmates who were looking at the different exhibits hurried over. They were all excited, so excited that two of the students accidentally climbed on Señor Gomez's work boots. They wouldn't give him any room.

"*¿Qué es esto, muchacha?*" Señor Gomez asked. He pulled a candy from behind Miata's ear and a dime from Ana's.

Miata and Ana accepted their gifts solemnly.

"What are you doing here?" Miata asked.

"This is my job."

"I thought you were a magician," Rudy replied as he pushed himself through the crowd.

"No, *joven*! That's just for fun." Señor Gomez gestured with a sweep of his hands at the reptiles behind glass. "This is my *real* job. I take care of this part of the zoo."

"What a great job! You get to mess around with animals and get paid for it."

"*Pues*, it's not exactly messing around," he laughed. He ran a hand over his face and said, "*¡Espérate!*" He jingled the ring of keys on his belt as he searched for one. He unlocked a door, disappeared for a moment, and then reappeared carrying what appeared to be a garden hose. But then the "garden hose" moved.

The students gasped, and Mrs. Diaz hugged the heads of two frightened children.

"Don't worry," Señor Gomez reassured them. "It's just a little, sweet baby."

"Cool. A boa constrictor," Rudy said as he drew close to Señor Gomez. He petted it with his thumb.

Miata edged back, stepping on Ana's shoes. She

74

held Ana's hand and would have taken off, but Miata had an image to uphold. Was she running for office or running away? She should be a brave leader.

"Can you do a magic trick with the boa?" Alex asked.

"Nah, not with this *hombre*," Señor Gomez said.

He let all the children pet the boa constrictor, which he told them was a month old. He let them feel the bulge in the middle of the snake.

"Feels strange," Miata said. It felt like a knot in a shoelace. "What is it?"

"It's his nourishment," Señor Gomez said bluntly. "He enjoyed a *ratoncito* for lunch yesterday."

Miata's hand leaped to her mouth as she thought of the mouse she had once owned. His name was Pelón, because he had a bald spot on the top of his head. She had got him at a pet store when it went out of business. Miata had owned him for three months before their bad cat, Midnight, chased it out of the house in the rain. That was the last she had seen of Pelón.

"Are you gonna show us a trick?" Rudy asked.

"A trick?"

"You know—some magic."

Señor Gomez rubbed his stubbly chin, then snapped his fingers. He left with the boa over his shoulder and returned a few minutes later with two turtles.

"They're so cute!" Miata cheered.

Señor Gomez let Miata hold one and gave the other one to Rudy. Miata cradled the animal gently, while Rudy knocked on the shell and said, "You home, dude?"

"I got *una buena idea*!" Señor Gomez said. "We're going to have a race."

Miata's face opened up into a smile. She looked at Rudy. He was now tickling the chin of the turtle, whose head had appeared from the shell. The turtle seemed to be grinning.

"A race?" Rudy asked. "I don't have a driver's license."

"No, *tonto*," Miata said. "The turtles!"

Rudy's face brightened. "Yeah, let's go for it. My turtle is a *bad* low-rider!"

"So is mine," Miata countered. She cooed at the

turtle. "Come on, baby. Do it for Miata. Beat this *mocoso!*"

Señor Gomez told the students to stand back, to give the turtles room. He made start and finish lines, using blue chalk on the cement ground. He told them the rules—that they could coax the turtles but couldn't push them.

"Fair deal," Miata said as she placed her turtle behind the blue line. "You better not cheat, Rudy."

"Relax, girl! I never cheat," Rudy said, spraying a mouthful of sunflower shells. To his turtle he said, "OK, on the word *Go*, do a wheelie and take off."

The turtles were lined up. The students named them after Miata and Rudy and chanted their names. The girls screamed "Miata! Miata! Miata!" The boys screamed "Go, dude, go!"

Señor Gomez raised his hand and said, "Ready, set, *¡Vámonos!*" His hand fell like an ax, and the race began.

The turtles took two steps forward, one step back, two forward, one back. Then Miata's turtle shot forward, taking three quick steps. Then it stopped and sat down, its head and legs disappearing into its shell.

"Come on," Miata cried. She tapped the back of the turtle, tapped and knocked. She looked over at Rudy's turtle, which was pushing ahead. For a turtle, it was speeding, hugging the ground as it advanced toward the finish line.

"Go, *vato*!" Rudy screamed as he tapped the top of the turtle's shell. "I'll give you some of my seeds if you win." He rattled his bag of sunflower seeds at the turtle.

Miata's turtle poked its head from its shell. It got up, stretched its front left leg, then its right, and took off—five steps without resting. Her turtle suddenly caught up with Rudy's. Then it climbed over Rudy's turtle, which had stopped and was as still as a stone.

"Man, that's sad," Rudy complained to his turtle. "Don't let her do that to you, dude!"

Miata's turtle pulled away. It was inches from the finish line when it stopped and turned around. It appeared to be looking at Rudy's turtle.

"Wrong way!" Miata screamed. "Turn around!"

Miata's turtle backtracked to press its nose

against Rudy's turtle. Rudy's turtle pushed itself to its feet, suddenly alive.

"They're kissing," someone yelled from the sidelines. "They like each other—Rudy and Miata like each other!"

"No sir!" Miata yelled, fists closed. "Huh, Ana?"

"Nah, they don't like each other!" Ana yelled above the noise. Her eyes were pleading for everyone to listen. But the students continued chanting, "Rudy and Miata! Rudy and Miata!"

Miata looked down at the two turtles. They were pressing their noses together. Yeah, they are kissing, Miata thought. She looked over at Rudy. He was stuffing his face with a candy bar, a splash of chocolate at each corner of his mouth. His hair was spiky, and his T-shirt was yanked and streaked with grass and food.

"I'm glad I'm not a turtle," Miata said.

Miata pushed away from the chanting crowd and was followed by Ana, her best friend and running mate. Arm in arm, the two girls decided to return to look at the laughing hyenas.

CHAPTER 7

Saturday morning. There were only a few days to go until election day. Miata sat before the cluttered desk in her bedroom, surrounded by campaign posters and buttons. She stirred the water of her five-gallon aquarium with a pencil. One of the guppies darted and blew out a single bubble that rose to the surface and popped.

"Come on," Miata said into the telephone cradled between her ear and neck. She was calling a classmate to remind her to vote on Tuesday. She had called Dolores, Alma, Sandra, and Apple, whose real name was Apolonia.

"Belinda?" Miata asked when a voice answered.

"No, it's her mom," the thick voice replied. "She's still asleep."

"Would you please remind her to vote for me—this is Miata Ramirez."

The woman said that she would give the message to her daughter and hung up.

Then Miata's telephone rang. Miata answered in an official tone, "The Ramirez residence." Then she heard that *quack-quack* of duck laughter. Miata sat up straight and pulled some loose ends of hair behind her ear.

"Who is this?"

"*Quack-quack.*"

"You think you're cute!"

"No. Rudy's cute. *Quack-quack.*"

"Are you a friend of Rudy's?"

"Better than a friend."

With this, the person hung up, leaving Miata repeating to herself, "Better than a friend. What does that mean?" Miata stared at the telephone. She picked up the receiver again and expected to hear the obnoxious *quack-quack* of laughter but got only the usual long *buzzzzzzzzz*.

When she heard her name being called, she left her bedroom and sniffed in the delicious scent of *chorizo con huevos*. She tried to get into a better mood. She skipped to the kitchen, where her father was already at the table.

"Buenos días," he greeted her, the sports page folded in front of him. "You been on the phone a lot, *mi"ja*." He sipped his coffee and asked, *"Pues,* so who's your *novio*?"

"Papi, I don't have a boyfriend! I was calling some girls to vote for me." She sat down, stomach growling, and clutched her napkin. She liked Saturday mornings. That was when her mother made tortillas.

"Dad," she asked, "you ever know anyone important?"

"Ever know anyone important?" her father repeated slowly. His eyes floated up to his wife, who was cracking an egg into the frying pan. "How 'bout your mommy? She's important."

Miata got up and hugged her mom's waist. "Mom is the best." She looked down at the eggs, now brownish red from the *chorizo*, and inhaled the flavorful smells of fried *papas*.

83

Her father sipped his coffee and said, "You mean someone well known?"

"Yeah." Miata returned and sat down, scooting her chair along the linoleum floor.

"Someone like a rock star or an actor?"

"Yeah, like that!"

"Someone like Eddie Olmos or Carlos Santana?"

"Yeah, Dad!"

"Like those *vatos* called Culture Clash?"

"Exactly!"

Miata's father tapped his wrench-thick finger on the table as he searched his memory. He finally shook his head and said, "Nah, can't say I have."

Miata's heart sank. She wanted to see if someone famous would endorse her campaign.

Joey came into the kitchen, still in his pajamas. His eyes were thick with sleep. He said, "Hi," and climbed into his chair.

Breakfast was now on the table. As Miata's family tore into the morning feast, her mom told her about a woman who had been mayor of a town in Mexico. It was Miata's *abuela*'s sister-in-law. The woman had been mayor three times and was responsible for educating the young people.

"A real mayor?" Miata said with her mouth full. She swallowed and drank from her milk glass. Her mind began to turn. She thought that maybe that woman could tell her something about winning an election.

"Yeah, in a *puebloecito* near Aguascalientes. That was way before she moved here." Her mother wiped her plate with a piece of tortilla.

"Can you call her for me?" Miata asked.

"If you want, *mi'ja*," Miata's mother said. "I think I have her number. But she's really old." Mrs. Ramirez got up and cleared away some of the dishes from the table.

Miata's father asked, "We're going to the *quinceañera*, *¿que no?*" as he picked up his own plate. They had been invited to celebrate the fifteenth birthday of a friend's daughter.

"Of course, but I'll let Miata visit with *la señora* for a little bit first."

After breakfast Miata and her father did the dishes, soapsuds climbing to their elbows. By the time they were finished, Miata's mother had arranged to see the woman, who lived nearby. Her name was Doña Carmen Elena Vasquez. Miata's mother said the woman was very happy to talk with Miata but would she please buy her some bread and Doña Carmen would pay her later.

"What should I ask her?" Miata asked. Now she was uncertain about meeting the woman.

"I don't know, *mi'ja*," her mother said. She was standing in front of the mirror in the hallway, dabbing her puckered mouth with peach-colored lipstick. "Come on. I'll give you a ride and you can walk home."

"Where are you going, Mom?" Miata asked. She pushed her face toward the mirror and glanced at her curls. She was starting to like her new hairdo.

"To Kmart."

Miata and her mother left, pulling away from the curb in their new used car, a Ford Thunderbird. They drove slowly up the street, the tires sweeping the fall leaves. They stopped at a convenience store to buy the bread.

They arrived at Doña Carmen's house.

"Don't let her pay you for the bread," Miata's mother told her. "Tell her it's a gift."

Miata got out of the car and eyed the small house, which was white with a toppled TV antenna on the roof. Geraniums, potted in coffee cans and milk cartons, lined the steps of the porch. A ceramic statue of *la Virgen de Guadalupe* stood in the middle of the lawn. On the bumper of Doña Carmen's old Ford LTD gleamed a sticker: YO ♥ JALISCO.

"Do I have to go by myself?" Miata asked.

"Yes. You wanted to meet someone important," Miata's mother replied through the window.

"Is she nice?"

"Of course she's nice. She's your *abuela*'s sister-in-law. She's family."

Miata looked at the house. A cat was now stretching on the steps.

"When you're done talking, I want you to go straight home," her mother continued. "We have to be at the *quinceañera* at three." She touched a button and the window slowly rolled up with a sigh. The Thunderbird pulled away, scattering some leaves and an orange-colored cat washing itself in the middle of the street.

Miata approached the house, kicking at the fall leaves. She walked up the steps, knocked on the screen door, and peered in. An old woman was

87

sitting on the edge of the couch. She was holding a lamp in one hand and a screwdriver in the other. A toolbox sat on the coffee table.

"Hello," Miata called brightly. "Am I disturbing you?"

"¿Quién es? Who is it?" the woman asked. She rose from the couch and unlatched the screen door.

"It's me—Miata Ramirez." She held up the loaf of bread. "I got it for you, Doña Carmen."

"¡Ven acá, mi'ja! Come in," Doña Carmen said in a singsong voice. She was a short woman, an inch taller than Miata, and walked with a slow shuffle. Her face was as soft as a pear, but her hair was steel gray.

Miata entered the house. A yellowish shaft of sunlight entered the corner of the living room, where a bookshelf sat. Portraits of the Kennedys and Cesar Chavez hung on the wall. A crucifix, made of bronze, hung on the wall.

"¿Cómo te llamas? What's your name?" Doña Carmen asked.

"Miata."

"Miata?" Doña Carmen regarded the young girl. "You gotta lot of curls."

Miata touched her hair. She wanted to explain the perm but thought the story was too complicated.

Doña Carmen told Miata in Spanish to sit down and apologized for the messiness of the house. She gestured to the toolbox on the coffee table.

"I'm fixing the lamp," Doña Carmen said. "It wouldn't close."

"You mean turn off?"

"*Sí*." She sighed and said, "So you want to be *la jefa*, the leader, at your school?"

When Miata nodded her head, the curls bounced about her ears.

"Your *mami* probably told you. I used to be the mayor of *mi pueblo*." She sat up straight, hands on the lap of her print dress. "Yes, I beat *mi esposo*, my husband."

"You . . . ran against your husband?" Miata asked.

"*Sí, muchacha*." Doña Carmen's eyes sparkled as she recalled her husband, dead now eight years. They had loved each other but had seldom thought the same way.

"*Pues*, he would argue, '*Vieja*, today is Tuesday,'

and I would say, 'No, *hombre*, it's Wednesday.' Then we would spend all week arguing if Tuesday was really Wednesday. That's how we were. We went round and round. Imagine! We lived like that for forty-six years until God took him away."

"So you ran against him for mayor?" Miata was now more than curious. She had spied a portrait of the couple on top of the television. They were as young as fruit on a tree.

"Yes. The man didn't want to advance. When we had a chance to hire some smart young women from Mexico City to teach in the school, he was against it. He said that the young women had city ideas that would make the children bad." Doña Carmen laughed and slapped her lap. "But you know what? Our children were already bad!" She laughed again and said, "No, they weren't *really* bad. They just liked to play."

Immediately Miata pictured Rudy and Alex. They just liked to play, too.

Doña Carmen explained how she had run against her husband because she had seen the future. She knew that one day the children of her town would need to advance, not stay in place.

"The days of working like donkeys were gone, *mi'ja*," Doña Carmen said. "And the *gente*—the people—could see this. So I won! I was the mayor for three terms!"

"That's great," Miata said. She was impressed and full of fire as she listened to Doña Carmen tell her about the new school they had constructed and the numbers who had gone on to the university.

"You're running against a *muchacho* at school, *¿que no?*" Doña Carmen asked.

"Yeah, this boy named Rudy Herrera."

"What is he promising?"

"Ice cream every day and more recess." Miata clicked her tongue. "Doesn't that sound ridiculous?"

Doña Carmen looked right into Miata's eyes and, it seemed to her, right into her heart. "*¿Y tú?* What are you promising?"

Miata looked away for a moment and bit her bottom lip. After listening to the old woman's story, Miata was afraid that she had nothing really to offer.

"I just want to do little things," Miata said.

"*¿Cómo?*"

Miata told her that her school was run-down. There was graffiti, broken equipment, a poor, muddy lawn, and no flowers in the flower beds. Her promise was to make things pretty.

"Good. I will help you."

"How?"

"I'll give you all the flowers and little snippings you need." Doña Carmen rose from the couch and pulled Miata by her arm. She led her through the kitchen and out the back door. They stood on the small porch overlooking hundreds of plants— geraniums, azaleas, rosebushes, hydrangeas, and jasmine.

"It's almost winter, but in spring, *pues*, we'll have *muchas flores!*"

"Yeah," Miata whispered to herself, as she pictured in her mind the fragrant jasmine waving in the wind. She also pictured the azalea she had planted, dotted with white flowers. "We're going to have a sweet-smelling school."

CHAPTER
8

Miata hurried into church behind her parents and Joey, who was wearing a tight-fitting tweed suit. Miata stopped to tug at an anklet sock, then skipped to find her place in the pews. She knelt, crossed herself, and sat down with her white-gloved hands in the valley of her lap. She wanted to break open like a flower and smile. She felt pretty because her mother had sprayed the cove of her neck with Passion cologne.

On the drive over to the church, Miata had asked if she could have a *quinceañera* when she turned fifteen. Her mother and father both said, "Maybe," which was as good as "yes." Excited, Miata daydreamed about her own party.

"What's her name again?" Miata whispered into her mother's ear. She had been told that the *quinceañera* was for the daughter of one of her father's coworkers who drove a cement truck. They were good friends, *compas*. They played on the same softball team and occasionally boxed in the garage.

"Juanita Lopez," Miata's mother whispered in return. She plucked at Miata's curls and said, "*Mi'ja*, they look pretty."

To this, Miata smiled and wagged her curls.

At the altar, between a scaffold of lilies, the priest was saying a Mass for fifteen-year-old Juanita, who was brilliant in a white dress. Her four maids—*damas*—were dressed in peach-colored chiffon dresses. Miata noticed that one of the *damas* was Veronica Torres, a girl from her class. She felt a twinge of jealousy. Veronica got to be in a *quinceañera* and she was only Miata's age, ten.

While the priest said Mass, Miata looked around the church. She eyed the boys and girls and recognized two of them from school. She eyed the parents, who sat fidgeting in their suits and stiff dresses. A baby started to cry, followed by another. When a man sneezed, another coughed and sneezed. Someone bumped a shoe or knee against the pews, and an echo resounded throughout the church.

I'm bored, Miata thought. She looked down at her gloves, which she peeled off. She became less bored as she admired her fingernails, which she had painted seashell pink with her mom's nail polish. Then, as she worked her gloves back onto her hands, Miata felt a tap on her shoulder, a tap that was like rain. At first she thought it was her imagination. Then the tap became harder, as when the doctor taps your chest and back during an examination. Miata turned and stared directly into the eyes of Rudy Herrera.

"What are you doing here?" Miata whispered.

"I don't know," Rudy said, shrugging his shoulders. "I think my parents know the girl."

"Where are your parents?" Miata looked across the aisle. She saw two adults smiling and waving at her. "Oh, I think I see them."

"My mom told me to tell you that she thinks you're really kinda cool."

Miata turned around when she felt another tap on her shoulder.

"You want some gum?" Rudy asked. He was holding out a single stick of Juicy Fruit.

"Rudy, you're not supposed to chew gum in church," Miata said, but grabbed the Juicy Fruit anyway.

"I'm not really chewing it," he answered. "It's just in my mouth." He opened his mouth, and before she could turn away, she saw the wad of gum on his back molars.

"Don't show me," Miata whispered. She looked over at his parents, who smiled and waved again.

Rudy went back to sit with them, and soon the Mass was over. Juanita Lopez marched down the aisle, like a bride, as relatives and friends stood up as she passed. Cameras and videocams caught her happiness.

Miata's family drove to a rented social hall for the dinner and dance.

"Who was that boy?" Miata's mother asked as the car rumbled over a smooth stretch of road. She was looking in the mirror on the visor, renewing the redness of her lipstick.

"Rudy Herrera," Miata said flatly. She offered the stick of Juicy Fruit to her brother. He took it and slipped it into his mouth greedily.

"You mean the boy you're running against at school?"

Miata nodded, and the curls on her head bounced.

"He looks like a nice boy."

Miata didn't reply as she peeked out the window from the backseat of their car. She spied Rudy's parents' car, a station wagon, in the next lane. She could see Rudy blowing a bubble as round as a soccer ball.

Miata's family arrived at the hall, their car tires crunching over the gravel. Her father parked away from the other cars because he didn't want to get dents on the car doors.

"You can never be too sure," her father said. "A little ding can ruin the looks of a car."

As they got out of the car, darkness began to gather like a knot in the east. They entered the hall and shook hands with Juanita Lopez's parents.

Miata's father gave his friend a full manly embrace, *un abrazo*.

"Is this *tu familia*?" Mr. Lopez asked. He was a handsome man with a mustache. He gave off the scents of cologne and coffee.

"*Sí, hombre*," Mr. Ramirez answered. He introduced his wife, Joey, and Miata.

"*¡Qué linda!*" Mr. Lopez sang to Miata. "What curls!"

Miata smiled until her eyes folded into little slits of light.

"*Y tú, hombrecito*," Mr. Lopez shouted. "Let me see your muscle!"

Growling, Joey flexed his right biceps. Mr. Lopez squeezed the bulb on Joey's upper arm and whistled through his front teeth. "What a guy!"

The Ramirez family made their way toward the dining area. A large cake towered on the table, with punch bowls on either side. A thin knot of guests hovered around the table drinking and talking, while others threw peanuts into their mouths.

"You kids go help yourselves," Miata's mother told them. She warned Joey, "And don't drink from the ladle in the punch bowl."

"What's a ladle?" little Joey asked.

"*La cosa* that pours *el ponche*," she explained.

The last time they had been invited to a party, little Joey, then six years old, had been caught drinking from a ladle. He had had a bad cold, and *mocos* like rivers had cascaded from his nose.

Miata and Joey hurried to the table. They worked themselves through the crowd. Miata poured glasses of punch for herself and Joey and was replacing the ladle when a hand grabbed it.

"Hey, girl," Rudy greeted her. He smacked his lips, pushing them out like a fish's mouth, and got ready to drink from the ladle.

Miata hollered, "Don't do it, Rudy!"

"What?"

"You know!"

"Oh, I say, how barbaric of me," he said with a British accent. "You're jolly right. I should be polite in public." He poured himself a glass, drank it quickly, burped, and poured himself a second glass. He wiped the froth from the corners of his mouth and said, "Ahhh, quite refreshing."

Miata pulled Rudy away, whispering in his ear, "I want to ask you something."

"Please excuse me, my friends," he said extrapolitely to those around the punch bowl.

"What's going on?" Rudy asked as Miata pulled him into the hallway.

"Have you been calling me?"

"Names?"

"No, dude, calling me at home."

"Nope. I don't even have your telephone number."

Miata examined Rudy's face. He seemed to be telling the truth.

Surprisingly, he then asked her, "Well, hey, girl, have you been calling me?" He hooked a thumb at his chest. The front of his shirt was a menu of the drinks and food that he had stuffed into his mouth. "Some girl's been calling *me*."

"Does she laugh funny?"

"Like a duck in water." He smiled and said, "She thinks I'm cute."

Miata didn't say anything to this. She let Rudy go but was confused. Who would make crank calls to both of them? Did they have the same enemies?

Soon a toast was made for Juanita Lopez, who blushed and tried to sip from her father's glass of wine. But he pulled it away and said, "Look at the girl. She thinks she's all grown up."

"Almost," Juanita said. She pressed her gloves across her moist brow. She smiled and waved to a friend in the audience. "Thank you for coming. *¡Saludos a todos!*"

She made a speech. Juanita told her guests she was now a young woman and doing well in school. She liked math and science and hoped one day to become a doctor. She told them she had tons of friends but—and she pouted playfully—no boyfriend.

"That's the way it should be," her father said jokingly. "We know about those rascals."

She finally said that she was glad she was fifteen because she could see how much her parents loved her. She hugged her mother and father and said, "I'm happy! Next year I can drive the family car." With her hands she made the motions of steering a car.

The guests laughed, and a few of the young women yelled, "Can we ride with you?" She smiled and said, "Sure, why not!"

Then an old man with sad eyes began playing music, and the guests began to talk among themselves. The old man warbled, and the evening became soft with his renditions of *"Sabor a Mí"* and *"Cielito Lindo."*

Miata stayed away from Rudy, though out of the corner of her eye she watched him. He ate all the peanuts, stuck a finger in the cake frosting, and played slip-and-slide in the hallway, even after he tumbled and cut his forehead. He just pressed a piece of napkin on his wound and continued running around.

A dinner of chicken *mole* was served with piping-hot piles of beans, rice, and tortillas. The clatter of dishes filled the room, along with talk and laughter.

Toasts were made in Spanish—one by Juanita's father, then by her *niña*, who told a story about how Juanita had once jumped off the roof to see if it would hurt.

"Did it?" a guest asked.

"Yes," the *niña* said. "Juanita came in crying and saying that she learned something today."

Then Juanita's baby pictures were shared. One was embarrassing—she was standing in front of a two-ring inflatable swimming pool with her diapers around her ankles.

Juanita pressed a napkin to her eyes and ran away giggling.

After dinner the tables and chairs were cleared away. An oldies-but-goodies deejay, who was Juanita's cousin Ricardo, spun the first record for the evening. It was Ritchie Valens's "Donna," a slow one.

Juanita danced with her father, then an uncle, then others. Finally everyone was called to the dance floor, and Miata jumped into her father's arms. They danced slowly, Miata's chin reaching near her father's heart—so close that she noticed a fleck of *mole* sauce on his white shirt. She looked down at the front of her own dress.

"Oh my gosh," she whispered to herself. There were three spots near the middle button—three small spots that began to magnify as she stared at them. She decided that once the dance was over, she would go wipe them off with a damp paper towel.

But at the end of the dance, Juanita's father announced into the microphone, "Let's pick new partners—one every twenty seconds."

When Miata turned, she was taken by surprise. Rudy was facing her and pulling on her arms.

Out of the corner of her eye she could see his parents smiling and waving.

"Come on, girl," Rudy said.

Suddenly she was dancing, one-two, one-two, with Rudy—her rival, the one boy who wanted to be president of their school. Miata's hands got moist.

When Mr. Lopez said, "Switch partners," Miata pulled away without thanking Rudy. She was embarrassed. She turned and found herself in the arms of an older woman who was only inches taller than Miata.

"I like your hair," the woman complimented her.

Miata smiled but didn't say anything. Her attention was on Rudy, who was dancing with Miata's mother. Her mother was laughing, and Miata couldn't help thinking that they were talking about her. Rudy is probably telling Mom about how I got caught on top of the roof at school, she thought.

"You have pretty hair, *muchacha*, so nice and

curly!" the woman sang. "*Pero* you got some *mole* on your dress."

Miata slowly lowered her gaze to the three spots on her dress. They seemed larger now, and Miata was even more embarrassed. She felt as if the whole party were looking at her, all wondering, "Who's that girl with the curls and *mole*?"

"Switch partners," Mr. Lopez crowed into the microphone.

At that, Miata escaped to the rest room, where she washed the spots. Only much later, when the cake was sliced and its sweetness danced on her tongue, did she feel better.

CHAPTER 9

On Monday morning, cold gusts of air stripped leaves from the trees and blew through the streets. The sky was dark and gray, even though it was 7:45. The birds huddled on the wires and chain-link fences. Despite the cold, Miata and Ana stood in front of the school handing out fliers, reminding their friends and classmates to vote for them. The girls took the fliers freely, but the boys said, "Nah, thanks anyway, we're voting for Rudy and Alex." They preferred more recess and Ice Cream Days to the drudgery of painting over graffiti and planting flowers and scratchy shrubs.

As Miata stood there, jumping from foot to foot

ause of the cold, she noticed that some of the
rls had perms. At first she thought they were
ats, but she was wrong.

"Look at Veronica . . . and Elena . . . and Ra-
quel over there," Miata whispered to Ana.

"Wow!" Ana whistled. "We've started a fad."

Miata saw this as a good sign. She figured that
they had the girls' votes almost for certain. They
slapped high fives but continued to hand out fliers.
They couldn't be too sure.

"Hey," a voice called from behind their backs.

Without turning, Miata knew it was Rudy.

"Say, girls," another voice called.

It was Rudy and Alex.

When Miata turned, her mouth dropped open
and out fell a Life Saver she had been savoring.
Her shoulders went limp.

Ana was shocked when she saw the boys. Her
fingers released the fliers, which flurried like the
autumn leaves.

The girls were facing two boys with perms. The
girls circled the boys, who modeled their hair and
snickered from the corners of their mouths.

"So how do you like it?" Rudy asked, touching

his hair with his hands. "Are we handsome or what?"

"Pretty cool, don't you think?" Alex crowed. His gaze followed the loose fliers and he said, "Hey, you're littering!"

"You're not making fun of us, are you?" Miata asked.

"What?" Rudy exclaimed.

"Because our hair got messed up with the perms!"

"*Chale*. No way," Rudy said. "Everybody likes your hair." Rudy glanced over Miata's shoulder at a girl running up the ramp toward the office. He pointed. "See, Patricia has a hairdo like yours, too."

Miata didn't have to turn to know that he was telling the truth. She looked at him. She had to admit that Rudy's perm was cute and, in her heart, she knew it was better than hers or Ana's.

"I did Alex's, and Alex did mine," Rudy said. "My mom didn't yell or anything."

"That's right," Alex said as he leaned an arm on Rudy's shoulder. "But my dad got upset. He said we look like a couple of girls."

"But you got him back," Rudy told Alex.

"Yeah—I pulled out some old photograph of when he was a hippie and had this really long hair."

Miata hurried Ana away when Rudy started rambling about how Miata had danced so well at the *quinceañera*.

"What's he talking about?" Ana asked while pushing a flier at someone on the way to class.

"Nothing," Miata answered. She paused for a moment before she added, "Except I went to a *quinceañera* and . . . Rudy was there."

"Was it his sister's *quinceañera*?"

"No, it was someone else's."

Ana bit her bottom lip, hesitated, and then asked, "You didn't dance with Rudy or anything, did you?"

"Yeah, I did."

"Did he step on your toes or anything?"

"Ana, let's change the subject," Miata said. She held out her hand, palm up. She felt a light patter of the first autumn rain. The lines on her palms began to fill and run like rivers.

Miata then heard the *quack-quack* of the laughter

that had been pestering her. A knot of girls, all cowering from the rain, had dropped from the monkey bars and were running toward the main building. Some of them had their coats over their heads. The *quack-quack* came again, but the girls were too many and too far away. Miata had missed her chance.

"Let's go," Miata said and hurried to the school buildings. The two girls zigzagged around school, handing out fliers. When the bell rang, they made their way toward their class. Miata couldn't help noticing a lot of perms—three girls side by side near the drinking fountain.

"Strange," Ana said to Miata, who nodded in agreement.

At their classroom they bent over the azalea they had planted the week before. Only a few miserable leaves still hung on for dear life. But Miata noticed one unfurling leaf, as green as "leaf green" in a box of forty-eight Crayolas. She felt hope, hope that maybe, just maybe, she might win the election.

The morning went quickly. Mr. Rios made his usual announcements about meetings and lost jackets and added a reminder about the next day's election. The classmates looked at Miata and Ana, and one of them cheered, "Go, girls, go!"

Lunch came and went. The day was wet and, even with the novelty of the election, boring. But during math, Mrs. Diaz discovered that their mouse, Vaca, had escaped from his pen. He was named Vaca because he was spotted black and white like a cow.

"Vaca's on the loose," Mrs. Diaz said, upset.

Miata glanced around the classroom. She spotted the mouse at the door, his long tail like a worm.

"There he is!" Miata yelled.

All heads turned in time to see Vaca's tail sweep around the corner and out the door.

"Go get him—Miata and Manuel," Mrs. Diaz yelled. "And the rest of you—sit down!"

Manuel was the fastest runner at school, so fast that he sometimes ran backward and still beat his opponents.

Miata and Manuel jumped from their seats and sped out of the classroom. Vaca appeared to do a wheelie on his back legs. He took off down the hallway. His tiny, leaflike feet churned under his fat, wiggling belly.

"There!" Miata yelled, and galloped after Vaca, with Manuel two steps in front of her. Manuel ran the length of the hallway and then spun around and raced toward the other end. Vaca had stopped in front of room 8, breathing hard, his whiskers quivering on his small pointed nose.

Oh boy, Miata thought. As her hands gripped the door frame, she peered into Rudy's classroom. Rudy was patting his curly hair. He was admiring himself in a small hand mirror, which was filled with the reflection of his eyeball. He spotted Miata looking at him. He swung around in his chair and mouthed, "What are you doing?"

"Chasing Vaca," she shouted.

She felt a yank on her sleeve. Manuel yelled, "He's going this way!"

The two chased after Vaca, who ran down the hallway and tumbled like a toy car down the steps. The mouse righted himself and ran out into the schoolyard, where the rain was coming down in windblown slants.

"Doggone it," Miata muttered. She tried to cover herself with her sweater, but Manuel took the

113

blunt thud of rain without covering up. They ran after the mouse, which leaped, wheeled, careened, and chugged toward the cafeteria/gymnasium. He disappeared through an open door.

The two kids followed and skidded into the building. They dripped rain. Miata backhanded the wetness from her brow and said, "We're only trying to help you, Vaca." She searched about as she tiptoed and led the way into the dark and cavernous room.

"Quiet," Miata whispered. "I think I heard a squeak."

The two of them listened. Miata took a step and looked down at her feet. Her shoes were squeaking from the rain. She sneezed and Manuel said, *"Salud."*

Miata found the lights and switched them on. The brightness made the kids rub their eyes. The students searched the room as they stood quietly. They heard a rustle and, when they turned, saw the VOTE FOR MIATA AND ANA banner waving as the wind blew in through the open door. The wind also blew in Rudy, who was wearing a baseball cap.

"What are you doing here?" Miata asked. "You're not supposed to be here."

"Yeah, I am," Rudy answered. "It's Ice Cream Day."

Then Miata remembered that it was Monday. Rudy was in charge of selling ice cream. He would put on a white paper cap and the cook's apron and bark, "Juicebars, Drumsticks, DoveBars, Popsicles!" Instead of handing back the change to his customers, he would flip it in the air for them to catch.

"So what's happening, girl?" Rudy asked.

"We're searching for Vaca," Manuel said.

"You mean, your *ratón*?" Rudy asked.

Miata and Manuel nodded their heads. They shushed Rudy when they heard a tinkle from the piano. They spied Vaca walking on the keys of the ancient upright.

"Hey, it's Beethoven," Rudy joked.

Miata tiptoed toward the mouse, calling, "Come on, Vaca. Nice *ratoncito*."

The boys followed, both snapping their fingers. Rudy sang, "We'll give you *queso* if you're nice. Otherwise, dude, it's the mousetrap for you!"

115

"Rudy!" Miata scolded her election rival.

"Hey, I'm only kidding."

Vaca eyed the three of them. His whiskers held a few fat drops of rain. His fur was bristly, and his nose was twitching nervously.

As Miata's hand rose to snatch him, Vaca took a step back. He jumped on top of the piano, just out of reach of their hands. From there he leaped onto the windowsill.

"The dude won't cooperate," Rudy whined.

"He's scared, that's all," Miata responded.

Manuel closed the lid of the piano. Then Miata and Rudy stepped up onto the piano bench and carefully climbed on top of the piano. Their weight made the wood creak and the roll-away wheels chirp against the wood floor.

"Come on, Vaca," Miata cooed. "Be a nice mouse."

"Yeah. Why don't you be like Mickey Mouse, dude? Cool."

Vaca stared at the two of them, his eyes black and beady. He wagged his tail and sniffed the air.

When Miata reached for him, he leaped from the windowsill and flopped on the floor like a water

116

balloon. But Vaca didn't explode. He flopped over and took off across the floor, with Manuel chasing him. The mouse raced into the cafeteria kitchen. Manuel screamed, "Stop, Vaca! We're only trying to help you!"

"Doggone it!" Miata yelled. "We almost had him."

The door blew open, sending in a rush of rain and Mr. Rios. He shook the rain from his coat, then stood with his hands on his hips, glaring. He approached them, his creased face running with rain.

"Miata! Rudy!" He shook his head sadly and wiped his face with a hand that was the size of a baseball mitt. "First the roof of the school and now this—up on the piano!"

"We can explain, sir," Miata said.

"You're supposed to be setting a good example at this school."

Rudy swallowed his chewing gum and nudged Miata. "Go ahead. Tell Mr. Rios."

"Well, sir, it's a long story," Miata started.

It was also a long walk in the rain to the principal's office.

CHAPTER

10

Mr. Rios let Rudy go, knowing that he had to sell ice cream. But he marched Miata to his office, where she explained how Vaca had escaped from his cage and how Mrs. Diaz had sent her and Manuel to catch the mouse. Mr. Rios tapped a pencil like a snare drum against a pile of papers on his desk and listened calmly, though Miata could see that he was steaming. The drumming became harder and harder, and the music of detention played in the air. When Miata finished, Mr. Rios reached for the telephone and called Mrs. Diaz.

"Yes, yes, hmmmmm," he said in his deep voice. He hung up the telephone, sighed, and bent so far forward that he was out of his chair and leaning over his huge desk. "Miata, I noticed that your fliers and banners are littered around the school."

She glanced nervously out the window. One of their banners had been stripped from the wall by rain and wind. A few of her fliers were plastered to the wet sidewalk. She knew what he meant: Let's clean it up.

Miata returned to her class as the dismissal bell was ringing. The first kids were tearing out of the classroom, including Ana, who screamed, "I'll be right back!"

They galloped toward the cafeteria/gymnasium to buy ice cream. Each of them was clutching fifty cents, eager to lap up sweetness at the end of a hard day of school.

Miata let the herd of classmates pass. She entered the overheated classroom with steamed-up windows.

"That bad mouse," Mrs. Diaz said playfully. She was at her desk stuffing papers into her tote bag. "Good luck for tomorrow."

"Thanks," Miata said in a near whisper. She had drawn a dark cloud of doubt into herself, wondering if she had any business running for school president. She turned and asked her teacher, "Mrs. Diaz, did you ever run for office?"

"Yes," Mrs. Diaz answered in a soft voice. "I ran for treasurer in high school."

"Did you win?"

"No."

"Did it make you sad?"

"Not really," Mrs. Diaz answered with directness. She walked over to Miata and gave her a hug that squeezed the air from Miata's lungs. She patted Miata's curls. "You'll get lots of votes, Miata."

"How do you know?"

"Because everyone wants to be like you. That's why they all got perms over the weekend."

Miata brightened. Maybe she's right, she thought.

The classroom intercom buzzed. While Mrs. Diaz walked over to answer it, Miata picked up her backpack and scolded Vaca, who was now sleeping in his pen. Wet flakes of sawdust stuck to his body. "Don't do that again, Vaca," she told him. Vaca opened a sleepy eye, eyed Miata, and closed it. The mouse was exhausted.

Miata met Ana on the playground. Ana was

wagging Popsicles in each hand. Her tiny mouth was as red as a clown's. She handed Miata one of the Popsicles and told her it was a gift from Rudy.

Miata was surprised but took a bite. The coldness hurt her teeth. She told Ana how she got caught standing on the piano, and Ana responded, "Wow! Did Mr. Rios get real mad?"

Miata shook her head.

When they finished eating their Popsicles, they started picking up their banners and fliers and stuffing them into the recycling bin. Miata couldn't help feeling that she was throwing away a little bit of herself. She felt as if something really important had come to an end. Finished, the girls parted, with the promise to call each other later.

At home, Miata was greeted by her mother, who called from the dining room, "¡Mi'ja, mira! Look what I found!" She was holding a small white box and trying to keep back a huge grin.

Miata guessed what it was but played along. She made her eyes big with curiosity.

"What is it?"

Her mother slowly opened the lid of the box,

which revealed a woman's finger. The finger curled slightly and wiggled on its cotton bed.

"¡Híjole! That's real scary, Mom," Miata said with a straight face. "Where did you get it?"

"It was caught in my car door."

"No!"

"¡Pues sí! I came back from shopping and it was sticking right out." Her mother closed the lid and turned her back to Miata, who knew that her mom was pulling her finger out from the bottom of the box. Mom was so cute when she tried to play practical jokes.

Miata sniffed the air. The aroma of enchiladas roamed the house like a ghost. And that's what they had for dinner, that and Popsicles for dessert. Miata ate her second Popsicle of the day, helped with the dishes, and then started her homework.

She was calculating 231 ÷ 14 when she looked up from her desk and noticed that one of her goldfish was floating on the surface of the water, its gills pulsating. She stood up and peered into the water. The goldfish's eye was big and frightening, and the fish was gasping.

"Oh my gosh," she said. "Bubbles is dying."

She left the room, called her dad for help, and went outside to cry in the garage. She stayed there for nearly an hour, playing with her old Barbie, which she had discovered in a box. She combed Barbie's hair with her fingers, used some spit to clean up her face, and changed her from a dress into a red-striped one-piece bathing suit.

"It's been a bad day," she told Barbie, who nodded her head and said, "But you're going to win tomorrow!"

Miata laid Barbie back in the box, muttered, "I wish you were right," and cried a little more. When she went back inside the house, her eyes were dry but red from crying her heart out.

After that, she called Ana to tell her that Bubbles had died and Pinkie, her other goldfish, was floating sideways.

The next day Miata rose from bed and gobbled a bowl of mush. Fog had blanketed their yard.

"Go for it," Miata's father said as he laced up his work boots. *"Buena suerte."*

"Mi'ja, we're all proud of you," her mother said.

Miata smiled and tried to feel good. She ate a second bowl of mush and readied for the big day.

She hurried off to school. She met up with Ana at the corner, and they walked to school yelling to friends and classmates to vote for them.

Miata noticed that more girls had perms. When she walked into the classroom, she was shocked to discover Mrs. Diaz's newly permed hair.

"What do you think?" Mrs. Diaz said, primping. Her face was lit with a big smile.

Miata smiled and gave her a thumbs-up sign. Some of the other girls in the class told Mrs. Diaz that she looked beautiful.

Right before first recess, the two fifth-grade classes voted. Slips of paper were handed out, and in less than five minutes the votes were cast. As the bell rang, everyone rushed screaming from the classroom to the playground.

"What do you think?" Ana asked as she and Miata left to join the others.

"I don't know," Miata said. "Maybe we will win!"

Miata looked around. The boys were on the lawn, playing soccer. Their knees were already caked with mud.

The girls examined their azalea, which was unfurling a few more leaves. The plant was on its way to recovery.

They walked around the school grounds. Miata wanted to ask friends and classmates if they had voted for Ana and her. But she knew that she would find out after recess.

When recess was over, the students returned to the classroom. Miata's heart was thumping. She kept gazing up at the speaker, knowing that at any moment Mr. Rios would announce the winners. The flag next to the speaker flickered in the wind from an open window.

They were working on their composition assignment, "Five Simple Ways to Help Save the World," when the speaker crackled, hissed, and finally popped. It came alive. Mr. Rios cleared his voice and said, "We found a pair of basketball shoes on the field. If you're missing a pair, please see me before lunch." The speaker went dead.

Miata searched the feet of her classmates. All of them seemed to be wearing their shoes. She shrugged her shoulders and continued her composition. She wrote on lined paper, "The world should plant more plants, really big ones so that they can eat up stinky car smoke. I hate it when you're standing on a corner and some stupid truck coughs up a lot of smoke. Number two, I think it's really ugly when people throw cigarettes from the car window. My Tío Frank used to smoke. When I went to the swap meets with him, he'd throw his cigarettes from the window. Then he stopped. Three, you know how animals have no place to live anymore? I would make a new country for them, like pieces of Mexico and the U.S., and put them together. Lots of animals from the world could go there and live. And we can also take a piece of Canada and the U.S. for animals that like it really cold."

Miata was thinking about her fourth point when the speaker began to crackle, hiss, and pop again. Her heart began to jump underneath her shirt. She looked up at the speaker, then at Ana, who was holding her breath.

"Good morning again, students," Mr. Rios said in his usual deep voice.

There was a howl of electrical noise and some rustling of papers. Mr. Rios clunked the microphone. Then he said without much ceremony, "We

127

have a new school president and vice president—Miata Ramirez and Ana Avila, from room six."

Everyone in room 6 clapped like thunder, and some shouted, "Way to go! All right!" Miata and Ana stood up. Their faces were lit up like pumpkins. Mrs. Diaz was smiling all the way to her gums, she was so proud of her two students.

"As you know, only fifth-graders vote," Mr. Rios continued, "and this was really close, thirty to thirty-two." There was a moment of silence before the principal added, "Rudy Herrera, please come to the office. I see your name on these shoes that were found."

The speaker went dead, and Miata's class resumed their work on "Five Simple Ways to Save the World."

School life was as sweet as Popsicles. At the end of the school day, Miata and Ana left the classroom arm in arm. They talked about what they would do first as president and vice president. They were happy. They saw Rudy running toward them.

"Miata!" Rudy yelled.

Miata noticed that he was wearing his shoes again. She noticed that he was covered with mud.

Even his curly permed hair was flecked with wet dirt.

"Congratulations!" he said, out of breath.

"Thanks," the girls sang together.

Rudy waited for his breath to return before he said, "Me and Alex voted for you."

Miata gave a look of surprise. "You voted for us?"

"Yeah," Rudy said. "We decided last night to go out for the soccer team." He hooked his thumb and pointed out to the field. "Alex wants to play goalie." Then he added, "You'll be a better president anyway."

Rudy extended his hand in congratulation. Miata shook it despite the slimy mud. Rudy ran away, leaving the girls looking at their dirty palms.

The girls walked to Miata's house to celebrate with big cups of hot chocolate.

CHAPTER
11

By December, Miata had pulled parents away from their televisions, made them button up against the cold fog that settled in the valley, and set them to work. Under Miata's leadership, parents painted over graffiti, fixed playground equipment, pledged money for a spelling bee, and helped spruce up a school in need of repair. In February, parents and students planted bareroot apple, plum, and apricot trees, all to be grown organically. Instead of selling candy bars during lunch, Miata argued, the school should sell fruit.

Doña Carmen Elena Vasquez donated nearly a hundred plants, including a maguey plant that would live a hundred years. Doña Carmen supervised the planting and even fixed her own blend of Mexican hot chocolate for the parents and children who worked. Señor Gomez the Magnificent persuaded the zoo to donate mice, hamsters, and three defanged snakes. Vaca was joined by a new mouse, which they named Conejo, or Rabbit, because it had buckteeth.

It was when Señor Gomez the Magnificent delivered the animals that Miata heard the *quack-quack* laughter once again. At first she thought it came from Ana, who was standing at her side. She was shocked to think that her best friend was the crank caller. Then when the laughter came again—Señor Gomez was pulling coins from his ears—she realized that the *quack-quack* was Ana's little sister, Alicia, a third-grader with Band-Aids on both chubby knees. Miata felt like yanking Alicia from the knot of students, she was so mad. But she played it cool. After all, Miata was the president and had to set an example.

"What do you think of him, Alicia?" Miata asked. Alicia smiled and said, "He's neat." Miata saw that Alicia was not really looking at Señor

Gomez but at Rudy, who was pulling bottle caps from his ears. He was trying to keep up with the magician, trick by trick. Now Miata understood. Ana's little sister had a crush on Rudy! Now she understood why she had made the anonymous phone calls.

Miata remembered that when she was a third-grader, she had had a crush on Richard Cortez, a fifth-grader. She had even given him a valentine card loaded with cherry cough drops stuck to the flap but hadn't signed the card.

"Yeah, he's neat," Miata agreed. She looked at little Alicia and as school president silently granted her an executive pardon.

That winter Miata was a busy president. She got a sporting goods store to donate soccer balls, even after the school team finished the season with a 3–7 record. A computer company came through with three free computers for the school library.

Miata and Ana were a good team. Once a week they got to speak on the school intercom and announce activities. When fights broke out, mostly among boys but sometimes among girls, they helped solve the problem. Ana started a girl's soccer team, and Miata arranged for her *folklórico* group to perform at the senior citizens' center.

The once-tame school roared with spirit. In March, Miata's spirits were bolstered when she received a letter from the White House.

Dear Miata Ramirez:

We are so pleased that young people such as yourself are taking the initiative to change the world through school environs. It suggests to all in our country a willingness to get involved. Unfortunately, the President is unable to provide you with strategies for winning a school campaign. He tells me that when he ran for the presidency during elementary school, he lost, as he says, "big time." The President does send his greetings to you and your school members.

Sincerely,
Michelle T. Rogers
Aide to the President

Miata thought the letter was pretty cool and allowed Mr. Rios to read it over the loudspeaker.

A few days later, as Miata returned home from school, her mother greeted her from the porch, where she was bundling newspapers for recycling.

"*¡Espérate!* Wait here," her mother said. The March sky was ribbed with a few white clouds, but spring was not far beyond. Soon the trees and plants would burst with flowers and scent the world again.

Moments later Mrs. Ramirez came out with a small white box. "Look at what I got," Miata's mother said.

Yeah, a finger, Miata thought. Joey had played the trick over and over until Miata had yawned with watery eyes. But when her mother opened the lid of the box, Miata saw a chrome-plated pen lying on a little pillow of white cotton batting. It was engraved: MIATA THE PREZ.

"Wow, Mom!" Miata said, nearly bursting with pride as she took the pen in her hand and wrote in the air. She weighed it on her palm and clicked it three times. She hugged her mother and then took out a piece of paper from her binder. She wrote, with a big looping action, BEST MOM IN THE WORLD.

"It's pretty," Miata said, and hugged her mom

again. For three months Miata had been asking her mom what kind of pen the president used. Now she knew. She faced the front window, where she could see her reflection with the sky mirrored behind her. Miata held up the pen and wiggled her head so that her still-curly hair bounced on her strong, square shoulders.